How to Speak Dolphin

Ginny Rorby

Scholastic Press / New York

To the memory of
Suzanne Byerley

All rights reserved. Published by Scholastic Press, an imprint of Scholastic Inc., *Publishers since 1920.* SCHOLASTIC, SCHOLASTIC PRESS, and associated logos are trademarks and/or registered trademarks of Scholastic Inc.

Library of Congress Cataloging-in-Publication Data available

ISBN 978-0-545-67605-2

10 9 8 7 6 5 4 3 2 1   15 16 17 18 19

Printed in the U.S.A.   23
First edition, June 2015

Book design by Ellen Duda

Text from *Little Dolphin* © 2012 by ImageBooks Factory BV; translation by Chronicle Books. Used with permission of Chronicle Books LLC, San Francisco. Visit ChronicleBooks.com.

The animals of the world exist for their own reasons. They were not made for humans any more than black people were made for white, or women created for men.

—Alice Walker, novelist

If the children don't go, there is no show!!!

—Ric O'Barry, director of the Dolphin Project

Never, never be afraid to do what's right, especially if the well-being of a person or animal is at stake. Society's punishments are small compared to the wounds we inflict on our soul when we look the other way.

**—Martin Luther King Jr.,
civil rights leader**

[Autistic children] have rich experiences, rich feelings, rich emotions, and these can be harnessed to help them learn to engage.

**—Kevin Pelphrey, director of the
Child Neuroscience Lab at Yale University**

* * * * * * * * * * * *

PART I

CHAPTER 1

Panama City, Florida

Born in a gush of blood, the dolphin calf's initial sense of the world is tail first into water colder than her mother's body. Her mother zips away to break the umbilical cord. The baby holds her breath out of instinct, not knowledge, and begins to drift away from the light above her into the darkness below. She's used to the comforting dark.

Her mother is back as suddenly as she departed and pushes her calf with her beak toward the surface and into the blinding brightness. Other female dolphins, some with calves of their own, are here when this newest arrival's blowhole opens and she takes in her first breath of the heavy warm air.

Inside her mother she could only arch her back and feel the confines of the womb with her flippers and tail. In this open water, she can swim freely, but instinctively she tucks herself in close to her mother's body and nudges one of her nipples. A jet of milk squirts into her mouth, then another, again and again until the baby dolphin is full.

Her mother will continue to nurse her for another year. During that time, the small community of dolphins roams the shallow waters of the Gulf of Mexico. It will be six months before the calf learns to follow her mother's lead and catch her own fish. She'll learn to follow boats because the humans sometimes share the fish they catch, tossing the scraps—skins and heads—into the water for the dolphins. The bolder dolphins are skilled at biting fish off lines, leaving only the head with the lethal hook embedded for the humans to reel aboard.

As summer approaches and the water warms, the dolphins travel to a spot where humans in boats from a place called AquaPlanet come to meet them. The first time the young dolphin sees these people squeaking and squealing at their arrival, she is frightened. She swims past the boat and turns on her side to watch. There are big humans and small humans. When the first of them steps off into the water, the calf darts away, but finds she is alone. Her mother, her aunts, and her cousins are letting the humans touch them.

She draws closer. Beneath the surface, she sees bony legs dangling uselessly from a puffy orange thing that makes the small human look like he is wearing a sponge to keep him afloat. The calf comes closer to inspect him with her sonar and can see his tiny heart beat as he flails the surface of the water with thin arms.

Curiosity gets the best of her and she draws closer. His face is distorted and red, and water, in big drops, drips off his chin. He lifts his arms and wails.

The dolphin starts to back away, but the boy sees her and stops the terrible noise. His head begins to waggle side to side like sea grass at the mercy of a current, and he reaches out to her with a small hand. She looks for her mother and sees her with one of the other children. This must be safe. Her mother would never lead her into danger. She lets herself float toward the child's outstretched hand.

When her rostrum touches the child's open palm, a shock runs through her; the child feels it, too. His head stills, his legs stop twitching; he smiles and makes a sound like water rolling across sand.

"This is that little dolphin's first visit to us," a human says. "You may have the honor of naming her," he tells the child whose cheek is now pressed against the calf's.

"What do you think, Owen?" says a woman in the water near the child. "You get to name her."

The child opens his mouth, and tries to speak. "Nor . . . nor . . ." His head falls forward, and he tips face-first into the water. His mother reaches and rights him. His eyes widen, and he starts the unhappy noise again.

The little dolphin puts her head just beneath the surface and blows puffs of air out her blowhole. The bubbles, one after the other, erupt on the surface, which makes the little boy laugh. He reaches for the dolphin. "Nor . . . e . . . e . . . een."

"He's trying to say Noreen." The woman smiles. "That's his sister's name. Her nickname is Nori."

"Nor . . . e," the boy says.

CHAPTER 2

Miami, Florida

Today is the kind of day I wish I had someplace else to go, like a friend's house. But a friend would expect to be invited to my house once in a while, and there's no one I can trust not to tell others what my life is like.

It's my fault. I haven't tried to make new friends since my first year at Biscayne Middle School. I'd invited a girl I'd just met over to swim. Mom was still alive, and when she left the room, that girl made fun of my brother. Adam's weirdness was just starting back then. The next day at school, she told everyone how "the retard" spent the entire time babbling and staring at his fingers, which he wiggled in front of his face, how he went stiff as a board when Mom picked him up, and screamed bloody murder when the phone rang.

Today Adam's having one of his tantrums, and I've shut myself in my room. Even with my door closed and my earphones on, I can hear his screams. By the clock on my computer, this meltdown is in its third hour.

I don't hear Don, my stepfather, knock, if he bothered, but I know he's opened my door because the volume of Adam's shrieks goes up.

He motions. "Come on."

"I'm trying to do my homework." Not true, of course, but studying is the only excuse that sometimes works.

"Lily. I need you to help me."

"Where's what's-her-name?" He hired a new nanny yesterday.

"She quit an hour ago."

I give her credit—she lasted a couple hours longer than the last three.

"Did you try his dolphin movie?" I ask. Adam would watch his scratchy and sticky DVD over and over all day long if we let him, so we usually save it for mealtimes. If he's watching it, he's more likely to eat what gets put into his mouth.

"I've tried everything."

I follow Don to the living room, where Adam lies on his back in the soft-sided, large-dog play yard Don bought at PetSmart. He's kicking and flailing his arms, and he's pooped his pants. Kind of like my life—the smell is awful.

Don puts his hands in Adam's armpits, lifts and holds him out so he doesn't get kicked in the stomach. "Take his pants off."

I almost gag from the smell. He's got poop down his arms and legs, up his back, even in his hair.

Stiff-armed, Don carries him into the backyard. I get the hose, which we leave coiled in the sun so the water will be warm. Adam's voice is hoarse, but he's still crying and kicking, trying to get away. I glance at our neighbor's house and see Mrs. Walden at her kitchen window. I think she had her gardener trim her hedge just so she could spy on us. She doesn't even pretend to look away. Don holds Adam's wrists together and suspends him so only his toes touch the ground. Even though Adam loves running water—fountains, sprinklers, the kitchen faucet—he hates being washed down with the hose. When the water hits his bottom, his shrieks rise to an earsplitting level.

The nozzle drips at the point where it's connected to the hose, so I feel the temperature change to cold and release the trigger. Don wraps Adam in a towel, carries him into the house and down the hall to the bathroom. I follow.

Don holds Adam pressed to his chest, one arm around his legs and the other pinning his arms to his sides as I test the water temperature and start filling the tub. Don's eyes are closed. I think from the pain of Adam screaming in his ear, but decide maybe it's because his heart is broken. I was seven and a half when Mom and Don found out she was pregnant and that the baby would be a boy. Don was so over-the-top thrilled that Mom looked at me and said *she'd* wanted another girl. She was trying to make sure my feelings weren't hurt, but it made me wonder if my real father had wished for a boy, too.

The tub is ready. I turn off the spigot, fold one of our big bath towels, and put it into the water against the back of the tub—something soft to protect Adam's head until he stops thrashing.

Don lowers him into the warm water. At first the volume of his screams goes up like we've lowered him into boiling oil, then he stops as suddenly as he started three hours ago. He begins to kick and swing his arms like he's swimming.

I stay with him until he tires of taking his bath toys out of their plastic bucket and lining them up on the side of the tub, knocking them off and lining them up again. I select a towel that's been rinsed in enough fabric softener to feel slimy, lift him out, and start to pat him dry. Sometimes he lets this happen unnoticed, other times he screams like I'm taking his skin off with sandpaper. I never know how he will react until it happens. Today, he leans over the side of the tub and flicks his fingers in the water while I dry his back and legs.

"Can I have a hug?"

Adam doesn't turn or hold his arms out like other kids. If he wants a hug, he'll back into my arms, and lean against me. He does that now, and I dry his belly, then his hair.

$$* \quad * \quad * \quad * \quad * \quad *$$

Adam no longer speaks, hates to be touched, and won't look at people, including us. Mom suspected he was autistic almost two years ago. Then she was killed, and I figured Don was too broken up to follow through with finding real help for him. Instead he went through a directory full of nannies and child-care facilities. Then, last year, Adam was finally diagnosed as severely autistic. I can't help feeling sorry for Don. He's a doctor but he can't help his son. His specialty is oncology. If Adam had cancer, Don might be able to cure him.

The first reaction of new nannies when they see Adam in his padded play yard is horror. But Adam is happier when he's confined. Maybe *happy* is not the right word—he's calmer in a tight space. Before Mom was killed she used to let him sleep in the bottom drawer of her dresser, surrounded by soft old sweaters and silk scarves. Don used to accuse Mom of coddling Adam, and after she died, he stopped letting him sleep in the drawer, and Adam went back to waking at all hours of the night.

Don's older than most fathers. I never gave that any thought until yesterday after school. Adam was asleep in his play yard. Don was in his recliner, leaning forward, watching him sleep, which is about the only time Adam is at peace. He looked up, saw me in the doorway, and put a finger to his lips.

I'd gotten close enough to see that his eyes were red. "What's wrong?"

He shook his head.

"Have you been crying?"

He didn't say yes or no. "I had to go downtown today for a meeting and I was at that traffic light at the bottom of the off-ramp. You know, where the men try to wash your windshield for tips." Don bowed his head. "I'm not sure you'll understand."

"You could try me."

"It was raining. Not hard, just enough that I had the wipers on intermittent, but this guy squirts my window and starts wiping. I tried to wave him off, but he didn't see me. Like Adam doesn't see me. The light changed and the woman behind me blasted her horn. That man got the same look Adam gets when he hears loud noises. I could see the pain it caused him, but he kept wiping my windshield, trying to get every drop."

I think about patting Don's shoulder, but don't.

"You know Miami drivers. Five seconds and the whole line of cars is honking. My wipers sweep across, catch the man's cloth, and snatch it away. He stood there, his face scrunched up in pain from the blaring horns, his cloth snagged by my wipers, and he couldn't move. I felt like I was looking at Adam twenty or thirty years from now." He looks at me. "What will become of him?"

"I'll take care of him."

"That's easy to say."

"I will. I promise." In spite of everything, I love my brother.

CHAPTER 3

I'm not sure I meant what I said about taking care of Adam. Since Mom died, Don has expected me to take her place. Instead of Adam's half sister, I'm supposed to be his mother. But if Don croaks tomorrow, here one day and gone the next, like Mom, I'm not sure I could take care of myself, or Adam. And there is my own life to think about.

Nothing worked out the way Mom thought it would when she married Don. He's a successful doctor and was really in love with her. I didn't have any feelings one way or the other about them getting married. My real dad was killed in the Iraq war when I was two, and though there were pictures of him all over our apartment, I didn't remember him.

After Mom married Don, we moved from an apartment on Kendall Drive near Mom's job as a nurse's aide at Baptist Hospital, to a beautiful coral rock house with an automatic gate and a swimming pool in Coconut Grove. It's within walking distance of Biscayne Middle School—a private school that Mom would never have been able to afford to send me to if she hadn't married Don.

Our new life seemed perfect and she and Don were even happier after Adam was born. I was, too. But by the time he was a year old, Mom started to worry something was wrong. Don said it was her imagination, and since he's a doctor, Mom stopped talking about it to him, but not to me. She went online and found a list of symptoms that fit Adam's behavior. "Watch, Lily, he doesn't look at me when I feed him."

"Maybe he's more interested in what he *is* looking at."

"He doesn't smile when I smile, and he's stopped responding when I say his name."

"Mom, Don says there is nothing wrong with him. He should know."

Mom looked at me. "He's wrong, Lily. I'm sure of it. Adam is autistic. He has all the signs. Look at this list." She took a ragged piece of paper from the pocket of her robe and handed it to me. I had to unfold it carefully since she'd nearly worn it out checking and rechecking his symptoms. There were little blue marks beside the ones she thought he'd shown so far: doesn't make eye contact, doesn't smile when smiled at, doesn't respond to his name or to a familiar voice, no longer sleeps well, doesn't follow an object visually, doesn't point or wave good-bye or use other gestures to communicate, doesn't look when you point things out, doesn't imitate your movements or facial expressions, doesn't reach to be picked up . . .

I refolded it and handed it back to her. I was only nine, but she watched me, waiting to see if I agreed with her. The problem was, I did, but I didn't want to believe it, either. There was an autistic kid in school. He had to go to special classes in the morning and be shadowed by an aide the rest of the day. He did weird stuff all the time, like cover his ears and bark like a dog when it got too noisy. At lunch he couldn't stand for his food to touch. If his aide or a teacher wasn't nearby, mean boys would stir his food together, or put a ringing cell phone next to his ear.

"What do you think?" Mom asked.

"I don't know, Mom. I'm nine."

"But you can see these all apply, can't you?"

"I guess."

At that moment, the kitchen phone rang. Adam began to scream.

CHAPTER 4

Don's hired a new nanny. Her name is Suzanne and she's been here a week; I'm hopeful. When I come into the kitchen Monday morning, she turns from wiping down the walls after feeding Adam and smiles at me. There's a spot of cereal on her cheek. I point to my own. "He got you, too."

"That child's a handful." She grins.

That is such an understatement, I can't help but laugh.

She laughs, too.

I like this woman best of anyone Don has hired. Her face is young-looking for someone Don's age but her hair is silver gray, so she looks motherly and grandmotherly at the same time.

Adam's high chair is jammed in a corner of the kitchen so he can't tip himself over when he rocks. Suzanne and I watch him swing his head from side to side, which explains the arc of cereal blobs on both walls. He's also banging on his tray with something round and hard.

I walk over and see it's the head off the doll Mom gave me when I was five. It had been given to her by her mother when she was little. It's my only treasure—the only thing special that I have of my mother's. I try to take it away from him, but he holds on with an iron grip.

"Give that to me." I pull up a finger at a time.

"You're going to set him off," Suzanne says.

"I can't help it. That's my doll's head."

"Aren't you past caring about dolls?"

"It was my mother's, and she gave it to me." My voice cracks.

"I'm sorry," Suzanne says. "It was in his toy box, so I thought it was okay for him to play with." She comes over and holds Adam's arm still while I pry his fingers loose. As soon as I have it, Adam starts to shriek.

"You go on and get ready for school, toots." She reaches in her apron pocket, takes out a pair of purple foam earplugs, places them in her ears, and goes back to wiping the walls.

I find the body of my doll in Adam's play yard. He's broken off her head, both arms, and a leg. I hug the parts to my chest and go to my room, furious with Don, who must have tossed it into the toy box.

I put the doll's head next to my computer and its body parts in the bottom drawer of my bureau. I'm about to close it when I see the corner of a little square book. It's the *Little Dolphin* finger puppet book Mom bought for Adam after one of our trips to see the dolphins at Ocean Reef, a club Don used to belong to. The book has a hole in the center where the fuzzy blue head of a dolphin sticks through the six thick cardboard pages. I remember her reading it to him over and over. I bring the book to my nose and sniff it like it might still hold a trace of my mother. It smells moldy.

There were times, especially when I was mad at Don, that I'd go to Mom's side of their closet and stand under the hangers, surrounded by her clothes, and smell her all around me. That was a long time ago. He's given all her clothes away and there is nothing left in this house that smells like her.

I carry the book to the kitchen, where Adam is still shrieking.

"Adam."

Suzanne's doing dishes with her back to me.

"Adam. Look at this." I hold the book up, catch his

chin, and force him to look at it. He stops screaming and reaches for it.

"Whoa." Suzanne turns and removes her earplugs. "What'd you do?"

"It's a book Mom used to read to him. I don't think I've seen it since she died."

Her eyes soften. "How long ago was that?"

I look at my feet. "Twenty-two months."

Suzanne walks over and hugs me. I'm tempted to melt into her arms, but I stiffen. What if she gets her fill of us and leaves like all the others?

Adam holds the book out in our general direction.

Suzanne releases me. "I'll read it to him, toots." She takes off her apron and pulls over the stool we sit on to feed him. "You finish getting ready for school."

CHAPTER 5

This morning, Don told me he's had his office manager research programs for autistic children and we're going to visit one after my school lets out this afternoon. He doesn't tell me why, after all this time, he's suddenly willing to consider a real program for Adam, but coming so soon after his encounter with the guy who washed his windshield, I think that may be the reason. I want to ask, but I'm afraid if I get too nosy, he'll change his mind. Whatever the reason, I'm excited.

The first thing I notice when we walk into the Cutler Academy's program for preschoolers with autism is how quiet it is. Carpeted partitions form small rooms within the neat and orderly larger room, and I hear women behind each partition giving instructions in low voices. There's no screaming.

At the only table not behind a partition, two boys a little older than Adam sit opposite a teacher. She glances up and smiles, but neither of the boys turns to look at us. They are following her example and using glue sticks and precut shapes of stems, leaves, and petals made from construction paper to copy a picture of a flower.

I glance at Don, afraid he'll bolt at the sight of boys making flowers, but even if he wanted to, he doesn't get a chance. An office door opens and a youngish woman steps out and closes the door behind her. She's pretty and tall—almost as tall as Don. I'm glad. He's going to have to meet her eye to eye, which will take away his surgeon-in-charge edge.

"Dr. Moran. You're early," the woman says. "I'm Elisa." She puts her hand out, shakes his, then mine. Her grip is strong and firm.

The older of the two boys at the flower-making table begins to sway from side to side and shake his head back and forth. "Daniel," the teacher says, "look at me." She catches him by the chin. "The leaves are next." She hands him a leaf and shows him on her picture where it goes.

"Please make yourselves at home, observe, ask questions," Elisa says when we turn back to her. "I've got a student in my office, but I'll be done soon."

"What's the point of having those boys make flowers?" Don says.

I have a feeling Elisa instantly gets where he's coming from. She smiles slightly. "It teaches them to focus and, in the end, to see what they've accomplished." She steps into her office and closes the door.

People respect Don, or at least his skill as a doctor, but I don't know anyone who likes him. And I bet Elisa's the first woman ever to do to Don what he does to everyone else. She finished with him before he finished with her.

I want Don to forget about boys making flowers and notice how quiet things are. There's a feeling of control here we never have at home. "Can you imagine Adam sitting still that long?" I whisper.

He's looking at the closed door, and doesn't answer.

The teacher says, "Now we need to put your flower in a vase." She holds up a piece of purple paper cut into the shape of a vase. "Look, Daniel. What is this?"

Daniel sways from side to side. "Paper."

"Is it a vase for your flower?"

"Purple." He begins to turn his head rapidly from side to side. The momentum of his head reaches his shoulders and soon he is whipping back and forth. A shock runs through me. Adam does this, too, when he's tired and frustrated.

The teacher reaches across and catches Daniel's chin. "Yes, it's purple paper cut into the shape of a vase."

"Purple."

Don looks at the ceiling.

"What are you trying to accomplish?" I ask, hoping whatever she says will keep Don from leaving.

"Autistic children can't generalize. I'm trying to get him to recognize that the paper is a symbol for a vase."

Don leans close to my ear. "Let's go."

"Why?"

"We're done here." He opens the door and steps outside.

I follow, but glance back. The teacher is watching us. "Please tell Elisa we couldn't wait. We'll be back." Like I have any say in this.

I get in the passenger seat and slam my door. "Why'd you do that? Adam needs help and that place is supposed to be the best."

"I don't see how it would benefit him."

"Of course you didn't see. You didn't look. You didn't give it a chance." I feel desperate—like if Don doesn't agree to allow Adam to go here, he'll never get the help he needs.

"This is my decision, Lily. I don't think that's the place for him."

"What kind of place *are* you looking for?"

He shrugs. "I'm not paying that kind of money for Adam to make paper flowers."

"You're not being—Watch out!"

Don pulls away from the curb without looking and into the path of an oncoming car. We're in a school zone, so the car isn't moving fast, but the driver still feels the need to blast her horn. I glance back, and she gives me the finger. *Whatever.* I look at my stepfather. "You're not being fair to me, or to Adam."

"He's *my* son, Lily."

"He's *my* brother, and the decisions you make affect us both." I suddenly wonder if I'm upset because I think he's doing wrong by Adam, or wrong by me. Do I want Adam to go to this school for his sake, or do I want him to go because it would give me a break?

Like he's read my mind, Don looks at me and says, "Are you thinking about Adam, or yourself?"

Since I don't know, I don't answer.

"Suzanne is working out," Don says. "And Adam seems to like her and is doing better. Let's leave well enough alone."

I pick my cuticle and want to scream, *You think Suzanne can get him to let you touch him, teach him to talk?* but as usual I wimp out and don't say anything.

CHAPTER 6

On Saturday, Adam wakes shrieking like he's been stabbed with a dull pencil. Nothing we try—the bathtub, his dolphin DVD, offering him a ripe avocado that he likes to eat with his fingers—works. After an hour of sirenlike shrieks, Don carries him screaming and kicking to the car. Driving sometimes works, but is always a last resort since it's like being sealed in a tin can with a train whistle.

Don learned the hard way not to put the windows down when Adam's having a meltdown. A cop pulled him over once and he had a tough time convincing him that Adam was autistic and not a victim of child abuse, especially since he's always got cuts and bruises.

I get in the back with Adam to keep him from escaping his car seat. "Where are we going?" I shout to be heard over Adam's screams.

"I don't know." Don looks at me in the rearview mirror with hollow eyes.

He drives south on the turnpike to Highway 1, then turns left onto to the Card Sound Road. Casuarinas and Florida holly grow densely on both sides of the narrow, two-lane road that goes to the resort of Ocean Reef and nowhere else, really. The sameness of the view and the hum of the tires finally lull Adam into quiet. Don sighs, but neither of us speaks. We're too grateful for the silence to risk talking.

Before Mom died, when Don was a still a member of Ocean Reef, we used to go down on weekends. As we reach the wonderfully high Card Sound Bridge, I remember how much I loved crossing it, swimming in the club's saltwater lagoon, and standing outside the clubhouse office, watching their two dolphins do tricks. Don pays the dollar toll and we start up.

"Look at the big bridge, Adam," I say. "We're going as high as the birds fly."

The car windows are tinted, which brings out all the different colors of the water: turquoise, green, and dark blue where it's the deepest. Adam lifts his arms like he's flying and rolls his head to look out. Not in time to warn Don, I see Adam's eyes widen with terror, and he shrieks.

"What the heck happened?" Don glares at me in the rearview mirror.

"Maybe it's the height."

"Okay, buddy." Don looks over his shoulder. "We'll be over the top and headed down in a second." He speeds up, and we crest the top, where the spectacular view is lost on Adam.

We start down the other side. "Here we go, Adam. Whee." I spread my arms.

Adam continues to scream until we pass a patch of open water filled with a hundred birds: wood storks, spoonbills, egrets, and herons. He quiets and stares.

To keep from upsetting Adam by going over the high bridge again, we have to take a long detour to get home. By the time we link up with Highway 1 in Key Largo, it's twelve thirty. Adam is rocking from side to side in his booster seat, and twice I see him put the tips of his fingers to his lips, which is American Sign Language for *eat*.

Last year I decided that if I could teach Adam the signs for *eat*, *drink*, and *toilet*, we might get out ahead of his frustration at not being understood and avoid a few tantrums. It took forever, but by holding his chin to make him look at me, I managed to teach him the signs for *drink* and *eat*. He never got the concept of using the sign for toilet *before* peeing or pooping his pants.

"How long is the drive home? Adam's hungry and so am I."

"About an hour and a half."

We can't stop at a real restaurant—the clatter of plates, tableware, and people talking would be too much for Adam—so when I spot a Wendy's, we order from the drive-through.

After we eat, Adam doesn't seem to be paying attention to anything except the fingers he's wiggling in front of his face until we're alongside a sign for a swim-with-dolphins place called Dolphin Inlet. There's a pod of bronze dolphins leading out from the sign. Adam turns in his seat as we pass, then starts to scream and kick his feet.

"Now what?" Don shouts.

"He saw the dolphins on that sign."

"Would you like to see the dolphins?" Don says.

I hate it when Don asks Adam questions he knows he can't answer, then, as usual, I feel sorry. I stay mad at Don most of the time because I don't think he's being fair to me, taking over my life to fill in for Mom. But then, I'm not fair to him, either. He's hoping as much as

I do that the urge for Adam to make himself understood will win over his refusal to speak. What if, just this once, he said yes, or even nodded?

As Don makes the U-turn, Adam quiets and leans forward, watching for the dolphins. His legs are now scissor-kicking, like he's swimming—but is he, or is it just a change in the rhythm of his constant motion? I look at the back of Don's head and decide to say nothing.

We come back past the sign and Adam squeezes his lips together and out comes a sound so much like the squeak a dolphin makes, Don nearly runs off the road. His head whips around to look at me accusingly. "Did you do that?"

I say no, just as Adam does it again.

The Dolphin Inlet driveway is gravel and crunches beneath our tires. Don pulls into an empty space under a palm tree, gets out, and goes to the back for the stroller.

Adam can't take his eyes off the sign and is doubled over looking at the leaping pod of dolphins, making it hard for me to get his seat belt and harness off. In the split second between getting him unhooked and leaning in to get his diaper bag, he squeezes past me and runs toward the sign.

"Grab him," I scream.

Don reaches for him, but Adam dodges him, runs toward the road, and disappears behind the board fence. I reach him a moment after Don does. He's looking up at the bronze dolphins and making the squeaking sound through compressed lips.

When Don picks him up, Adam screams and kicks, and delivers a blow to Don's stomach that almost knocks the wind out of him.

"Adam. Look at me." I grab his feet. "Look at me. If you stop, we'll go see the real dolphins. Okay?" His legs relax. "For that to happen, you have to stop screaming. Screaming will scare the dolphins." I hold my hand out to him. "You have to take my hand and walk slowly. Do you understand?" Of course he doesn't take my hand, but he doesn't pull away when I take his. Don puts him down and rubs the spot where Adam kicked him.

The parking lot stretches down to the bay, where another tall fence blocks the view of the water. I hear a whistle and turn in time to see two dolphins leap into the air, somersault, then splash back into the water. The sight gives me gooseflesh. Dolphins have become so much Adam's thing that I'd forgotten how much I used to love seeing them at Ocean Reef. I never missed a show, and once, on a rainy Saturday when no one else was around, I crawled under the wooden bridge that crossed one end of their lagoon, and sat on the coral rocks to watch them until I heard Mom calling. Before that day, I thought they chose to live in that lagoon, but under the bridge was a net that kept them from swimming out into ocean.

* * * * * *

The girl behind the desk in the Dolphin Inlet office glances up when we come in, then at the clock. "You're early. The next swim is at two."

Don and I both turn toward the clock. It's one fifteen.

"We were driving by and saw the sign. My son . . . my son loves dolphins. Could we just take him down to look at them?"

"You can at two. This is their break time."

Adam pulls free of my hand and runs over to a display of stuffed toy dolphins. He starts taking them out and lining them up on the floor. The girl stands so she can see over the counter to watch him.

"I'll put them back," I say.

"And we'd like to buy one." Don takes out his wallet. "Look, could we pay a little extra to walk down and let him see them? He's a little restless and won't last forty-five minutes."

"I'm sorry. I can't let you do that."

I can tell Don is about to turn surgeon-in-charge on her. "Young lady—"

Adam has all the stuffed dolphins lined up and is squeaking at them.

"My brother is . . . autistic. He won't be calm much longer," I say as nicely as I can. "Could we please take him down to look at the dolphins?"

"Autistic! You're at the wrong place. You want the Largo Center. I can show you on a map. It's very close."

"Why is that better than here?" Don says.

The girl's face softens even though his tone was brusque. "This is just a swim-with opportunity. Largo has a dolphin-assisted therapy program for disabled children."

The word *disabled* hangs in the air. I glance up at Don. Only his eyes have changed, crinkling in the corners like he's been punched. He turns to watch Adam realigning the row of stuffed dolphins, then exchanges the twenty he'd taken from his wallet for a hundred-dollar bill. "We'll take them all."

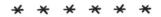

Back in the broiling hot car, I give Adam one of the dolphins and toss the bag with the others into the back of the SUV. "Are we going to the other place?"

Adam shakes the dolphin back and forth, squeaks, and rocks his own head side to side.

"Don?"

"What?"

"Do you want to try the other place?"

"No."

I'm disappointed. I know this isn't a happy family road trip, but it's nice being out of the house, and *I* would like to see the dolphins. "How come? She said it wasn't far."

"He's happy enough with the stuffed ones." Don starts the engine, throws it in reverse, glances in the rearview mirror, and steps on the gas. Gravel pelts the underside of the car as he peels out of the parking lot.

CHAPTER 7

I'm at my desk the following Saturday morning when Don appears in the doorway and raps on the frame. "You busy?"

I'm surprised he asked. "Not really."

He walks over. "What are you doing?"

I hold out my left hand. "Putting on polish."

"Black?"

"Yeah. A lot of kids wear black nail polish."

"I don't like it."

"Too bad. I do." My heart goes flub, flub. I never sass him.

He watches me paint my thumb, then says, "I was thinking maybe we'd go down to that dolphin place."

"Which one?"

"The therapeutic one."

"Really? What made you change your mind?"

"I haven't changed my mind. I'm pretty sure the therapy is a gimmick, but it can't hurt to check it out. I cut a deal with the owner. She's going to let Adam swim with the dolphins whenever we get there."

"What kind of deal?"

He smiles, holds his hand up and rubs his thumb back and forth across his fingertips.

"You gave her money?"

"A donation."

"How much?"

"None of your business."

I hate that he manages to find a shortcut when he expects other people to follow the rules. It's like he's always butting in line.

He sticks his head around the door again. "He'll need a swimsuit and so will you."

* * * * * *

After Adam got away from us at Dolphin Inlet, Don went online and bought a Mommy's Helper Kid Keeper harness and leash, which I wrestle Adam into like he's our pet dog before I open the car door at the Largo Center.

We take an elevator to the second floor. French doors along the back wall make the large room bright and sunny. A girl a couple years older than me sits at the table near the entrance to the gift shop. Her hair is wet.

"I'm Dr. Moran," Don says, clearly assuming she's expecting us.

She looks at him, then at Adam straining against his leash, trying to get to a fish tank in the center of the room, then at me. I stare at her so she'll know I don't care what she thinks of us.

She stands up. "I'm just an intern. I'll get someone to help you."

She crosses the room to a row of desks. From the other direction, a girl passes us, balancing two bowls of finger paints.

Don's expression as he watches the finger-paint girl disappear down the hall is the same as when the boys were making paper flowers.

A thin, frazzled-looking woman comes out of a back office. Don's attention is on Adam, who has his hands wrapped around the leash and is trying to yank it out of my fist. He doesn't see the intern point to us, or see the woman's face harden. Her resentment at being offered more money than she could afford to refuse, so his kid can bypass whatever he considers unnecessary, is clear on her face.

"Dr. Moran." She extends a wrinkled brown hand. "Nice to meet you. I'm Debra." Her voice is flat.

Don hesitates, then shakes her hand. "That's my

son, Adam." Adam is now on his hands and knees, squeaking at the pile of stuffed dolphin toys just like the ones Don bought him in the other gift shop. "And this is Lily." Then he thinks to add, "My . . . daughter."

She nods to me. "So, Dr. Moran, I'm grateful for your generous donation, but I'm not sure what you hope to accomplish outside the parameters of the program."

"I've read some amazing claims about dolphin therapy, and he"—Don nods toward Adam—"seems to have some interest in dolphins, but I'd like to test the waters, so to speak."

"Do you think the claims seem too good to be true?"

"Frankly, yes."

"Then why are you here?"

Don's whole body tenses and I flinch, expecting him to explode like a grenade, but when he answers, his voice is totally calm. "Adam doesn't speak. He doesn't communicate at all. I'm hoping, if the claims are valid, for a breakthrough."

"I can tell you, Dr. Moran, that's not going to happen. He's an autistic child and he will grow up to be an autistic adult. With therapy—extensive therapy—he will eventually talk." She looks at Adam. "In my twenty-five years of doing this, I've never seen a nonverbal kid speak because of dolphin therapy. And, by the way, he *is* communicating—in his own way. You have to know how to listen."

Don's jawbones are practically poking through his cheeks. "Really?" His tone is patronizing.

Debra hands attitude right back to him. "Certainly. If you ask him if he wants yellow, blue, or green and he selects blue, he's communicating."

I duck my head to hide that I'm smiling. "Adam knows two signs," I say.

"What do you mean?" Don snaps, taking his anger at Debra out on me.

"I taught him the sign for eat and for drink."

"What kind of sign?"

"American Sign Language. This is *eat*." I bring my clumped fingers to my lips. "And this is *drink*." I make an imaginary glass, and tip it to my mouth.

"What does he need sign language for? He's not deaf."

"Anything that aids communication in autistic children is a good thing," Debra says. "Sign language is very helpful."

Don hands me Adam's swimsuit; Debra points to the bathroom on the other side of the room. I carry Adam in, screaming and kicking, and shut the door.

CHAPTER 8

Debra leads us through the French doors and out onto the balcony overlooking the dolphin enclosure, which has been dynamited out of the coral rock foundation. The water is dark green and empty-looking. It reminds me of the dolphin enclosure at Ocean Reef. And like Ocean Reef, a submerged fence keeps the dolphins from swimming out into the adjacent canal and escaping to the open ocean.

A wooden dock runs the length of the fence. Anchored to the dock are three rafts, the first of which has a canopy for shade, a chair, a Hula-Hoop, a beach ball, and a bucket of fish. There's a snorkel and mask, two black life jackets, one for me and one for Adam, and a selection of swim fins. I'm the one who is going into the water with Adam, and though I'd never admit it to Don, I'm so excited my heart is pounding. I've wanted to swim with dolphins for as long as I can remember.

A flattened circle forms on the surface of the pond, then another. Paw prints, the Ocean Reef trainer told me once, made by dolphins traveling just beneath the surface. I tighten my grip on Adam's leash, but the water bubbling out of a huge, coral rock fountain has his full attention.

Debra leads the way down the flight of stairs to the dock. Don follows, and I try to take Adam's hand, but he jerks it away and clamps it in his armpit. Don has stopped midway down and looks up at us.

"He's watching the fountain." I kneel and turn Adam to face me. His body rotates, but his eyes stay on the fountain. "Adam, look at me. Do you want to see a dolphin?"

His head turns, but his eyes search and find something to stare at over my left shoulder. If Adam was normal, I'd think it was because he can't stand the sight of me, and I'd be hurt. Sometimes I feel like that anyway, even though I know, for whatever reason, eye contact is painful for him.

"If you give me your hand, we'll go see a real dolphin."

He pulls his right hand from under his left armpit and holds it up. It's damp and hot when I take it.

We're halfway down when two dolphins pop up by the raft where Don and Debra wait for us. Adam squeals and tries to run. I jerk his arm. "Hold still. You'll scare them away if you aren't quiet."

With his other hand on the railing, he takes each step carefully, knees bent like he's sneaking up on them, all the time doing his dolphin sound. I feel my heart break open like an egg. What is it about dolphins that can reach him when nothing else can?

This is not the first time I've wondered what a four-and-a-half-year-old remembers about being one or two or three. Is he drawn to anything dolphin because he remembers Mom and the Ocean Reef dolphins? Does he remember not being autistic, and is that part of the frustration he lives with? When thoughts like this come to me, I remember Mom trying to keep my father alive in my memory, and I worry that over time I will forget her, too, like I have forgotten him. I guess that's the reason I practice remembering her—like studying for a test. I do it for myself, but I'm also the keeper of her memory for Adam, in case he ever asks.

At the bottom of the steps, I release his hand but hold on to the leash. If it weren't for the waist-high chain-link fence running the length of the walkway, Adam would have launched himself into the water. His little legs churn as he runs toward the dock with me loping behind him. When he gets to the raft, Don throws an arm out to stop him from leaping into the water, but Adam ducks under it, flops on his belly, and pulls himself to the edge.

Don drops his arm and looks at Debra, whose tough, thoroughly pissed-off exterior melts. "That's exactly how my son was the first time he met a dolphin," she says.

Two fins cut the water, and both dolphins pop up in front of Adam. He laughs and holds his arms out. One of the dolphins comes right up and fits his snout against Adam's left eye socket. Adam giggles and squeaks.

The other dolphin bobs its head and squeezes a whistle out its blowhole.

Don closes his eyes and pinches the bridge of his nose, making me wonder if he feels like crying, too.

It's hard to pry Adam's hands loose from the edge of the raft and stand him up long enough to get him out of his Kid Keeper harness and into a life jacket. I let Don deal with it, pull on my own life jacket, adjust the dive mask, and slip into water as warm as a bath. Immediately, I feel the pressure of a dolphin passing and put my face in the water to look for it. I see one of the dolphins disappear into the dark water, but the other slides up beside me on the surface. I hesitate long enough to glance at Debra to see if I'm allowed to take the offered fin, but she's checking the fit of Adam's life jacket. I fold my hand around its dorsal fin and feel the force of its tail sweep down, then up, and the pressure of water against my chest. When I put my head back and laugh, the dolphin picks up speed until we are ripping through the water so fast my chin throws up a rooster tail. The dolphin drags me the entire length of the pool and back, then sinks out from beneath me when we're an arm's length from the raft.

"Oh, my god." I shake my hair out of my face and grin at Don. Finally, the word *awesome* means something really awesome. "That was so much fun."

Adam is trying to pull free of the hold Don has on his wrist. "This is supposed to be about your brother."

Debra looks startled.

I feel punched. "When isn't it?" I mumble.

The dolphin Debra calls Squirt surfaces and upends beside me. I love the feeling of hanging in the water side by side, with an eight-foot-long bottlenose dolphin, watching the two big land mammals wrestle the little one. I lay my hand on Squirt's cool gray skin. When he doesn't move away, I lean and kiss his cheek.

Adam wails and stamps his feet, then falls to his knees. "Why don't you let him go?" I say.

"I think the dolphins go too fast for him." Don's tone is softer, the only apology I'll get.

"Don't worry," Debra says. "The dolphins know exactly how to behave with each client. They'll be gentle."

Don places his hands in those hot armpits and lowers Adam over the side. Adam puts his face in the water, kicks his feet, and propels himself toward me, blowing bubbles on the surface. When he reaches me, he turns and puts his back against my chest. I close my eyes against the pain of his trust in me.

Squirt drifts over and places his snout against Adam's cheek. Adam squeaks. Squirt bounces his head and answers him. They take turns making dolphin sounds, a conversation the rest of us can't understand.

Debra tells me to try sticking my legs out, toes turned up. I hold Adam, and Squirt, the more playful dolphin, pushes us around the pond with his snout pressed to the soles of my feet. When Debra tosses the beach ball into the pond, the other dolphin, Bella, goes after it and uses her snout to pitch it to us. Adam makes a fist and hits at it, but misses. Bella pushes it closer, and he connects the second time. On a sign from Debra, Bella dives, comes up under the ball, and whacks it back to us with her tail.

Each time the dolphins interact with us, they go to the raft for a fish reward, then Debra signals them to return and play again.

When Squirt snaps his jaws together, creating a jet of water, I realize where he got his name. It makes Adam giggle. At Debra's signal, the dolphin rolls on his back for a belly rub. I reach to go first to show Adam it's safe, but he beats me to it and places his small hand on the dolphin's chest. Squirt lies still in the water, letting Adam stroke him until he has to breathe, then he upends and holds his flippers out like a pair of arms. Adam turns and backs up against the dolphin.

I look at Don, but he doesn't know how monumental this is. I've never told him it's the only way Adam allows himself to be hugged, because Adam has never let his father hug him.

"Are you ready for a ride, Adam?" Debra signals Bella, who comes up beside me to let me wrap Adam's hands around her dorsal fin. When he's got a firm grip, she drags him slowly across the pool, makes a wide turn, and brings him back to me.

Adam splashes Squirt, and Squirt twirls, flippers held out so they throw arcs of water over both of us. Adam giggles, spreads his arms, and kicks his little legs awkwardly, trying to turn fast enough to splash Squirt in the same way.

When they tire of that, Bella launches into a game of hide-and-seek, popping up behind Adam no matter which way he turns. He shrieks with laughter. The harder he laughs, the sadder I feel that I haven't seen Adam this happy since he was a baby—before whatever happened to him happened.

We've been in the water for the full hour. Adam's lips are blue and he's shivering. I've got chill bumps from head to toe, and the skin on my fingers is white and wrinkled. When Don signals me to bring Adam to the raft, I begin working us in that direction. Getting him out and away from the dolphins is going to be a nightmare. Squirt, the one who has played with us the most, puts his snout against the bottom of Adam's foot and pushes us around in circles, all the while edging us toward the raft. Adam's back is to Don when he reaches over and lifts him out of the water. Adam screams and kicks to get free.

Debra signals the dolphins, and they disappear. She steps around the bucket of fish and catches Adam's feet. She stops his head from shaking by holding his chin pinched between her thumb and forefinger. "Adam, look at me. You are scaring the dolphins." She points to where they have surfaced at the far end of the pond. "They don't like children who scream. If you and the dolphins are going to be friends, you have to be calm and quiet."

Adam doesn't look at her, but he's listening and stops screaming.

"The last thing we do when we are done playing with the dolphins is give them the rest of their fish," Debra says. "If you are quiet, you can feed them. Can you do that?"

Adam brings a clump of fingers to his lips: the sign for eat. I'm amazed and look at Don. Debra—a stranger—asked Adam a question and for the first time ever, he answered. Even if Don doesn't recognize that Adam signed an answer, he has to see this place is good for him—makes him happy.

"Good boy." Debra signals the dolphins. They dive and pop up a moment later beside the raft.

Don puts Adam down, and Debra places the smelly bucket of dead fish beside his leg. "I'll show you how to do it." She lifts a fish by the tail and holds it over the water. Squirt opens his mouth in a wide, toothy smile, and she drops it down his pink throat.

Adam squats, picks up a fish, holds it out to Bella, and lets it go when the dolphin opens her mouth.

"Perfect," Debra says.

After the bucket is empty, Debra sends the dolphins away, and Adam lets me dry him off. He even holds his arms up so I can put on his T-shirt, and he lets me take his hand as we walk the dock. At the bottom of the stair-case, he pulls free and runs to the fountain, stands on his tiptoes, and flicks the water with his finger. It's then I notice a small pen around the corner. I walk over to look inside. It holds a lone sea lion. There's a lot of algae growing on the netting that separates this pool from the dolphin pond, which is probably the reason I didn't notice it when I was on the other side with the dolphins. The sea lion is swimming back and forth like a tiger pac-ing its cage. Her head turns so no matter which direction she's swimming, she's looking out at the larger body of water.

"Adam, come look at the sea lion."

He leaves the fountain, comes to stand beside me, and curls his fingers through the chain-link fence. Adam doesn't turn his head, and I don't see his eyes track the sea lion's back-and-forth pattern, but after a couple of minutes, he begins to rock from side to side. I watch my brother and the sea lion and am suddenly angry, but before I can think of why or at whom, Adam lets go of the fence and begins to shake his hands like he does when he can't make us understand what he wants. I wonder if he's feeling the sea lion's distress, if he's feel-ing empathy—an ability supposedly lost to autistic kids.

✳ ✳ ✳ ✳ ✳ ✳

When Adam and I come out of the bathroom in our dry clothes, Don is buying two Largo Center T-shirts—one for Adam and one for me.

Debra is standing by the elevator with her arms crossed over her chest, clearly waiting for us to leave.

Don hands me the T-shirts and says to Debra, "I think this looks very promising and Lily will be out of school in a couple of weeks, so I'd like to set up a schedule for the rest of the summer."

Before I can say wait a minute, do I have a say in this, Debra says, "For the full program?"

"No. I'd prefer that you let Adam come down for private sessions with the dolphins."

Debra shakes her head. "I made an exception today because our five-day programs don't start until next week. If Adam comes back, he needs to participate in the entire program with our trained therapists. Those sessions include classroom art projects, massage, music, and time in the water with the dolphins."

Don gets a smirky look on his face.

Debra sees it, too. "We appreciate your donation, and I think our program would help Adam, but you only bought your way into one exception."

"I have a practice—patients with cancer. I can't come down to the Keys for five days."

"I'm aware of your situation, but there's nothing I can do about it. Most of the upcoming sessions are full anyway."

"We'll come on Sundays, if that's more convenient."

"Today was a one-time concession, Dr. Moran. Your son clearly has a connection to dolphins, but he also needs therapy to address his autism issues."

"How much do you want?"

Debra's jaws work beneath her sun-damaged skin. "Please leave, Dr. Moran. This is not the place for you." She turns and walks away.

I'm furious. He walked out of Cutler Academy and now, thanks to him acting like a pompous butthead, we can never come back here. And—not that it matters now—he didn't ask me if I was willing to give up every Saturday for the rest of the summer—which I would have, to swim with the dolphins again.

I watch Debra march off, then turn to Don. "How'd you let that happen? And did it occur to you I might have other plans on Saturdays?"

He looks at me. "Like what? Another couple of weeks and you'll have all day, every day, to do whatever you want to do. Saturday and Sundays are Suzanne's days off and they should be for Adam."

"Every day is for Adam," I snap.

"What difference does it make? That woman is never going to let us come back."

"I don't care. You should ask me first before you plan the rest of my life."

Don doesn't have a clue about my friends, or lack of friends. He's never bothered to ask. Even if I don't have kids my own age to hang with, I should be free to decide what I do on weekends. Don's blown off the Cutler Academy and, now, Adam's chance to see if dolphin therapy works.

Nothing's going to change—for Adam, or me.

PART II

CHAPTER 9

Panama City, Florida

Nori lies in water so shallow it barely covers her flippers. Her back is exposed to the hot sun and her skin has begun to blister. The wash of the waves rocks her back and forth, but not for long. The tide is going out.

Her mother stays close, clicking frantically and whistling Nori's name, encouraging her to try for deeper water, but Nori is too weak. They both pick up the sound of a motor and recognize it as one of the boats from AquaPlanet bringing children to this island to swim with the dolphins. Her mother races toward it, changes her mind, returns to Nori's side, nudges her and clicks, backs into deeper water, and turns to meet the boat.

"Isn't that Nori's mom?" One of the women points at the dolphin, then shades her eyes. "Where's Nori? They're always together."

The humans gather on the side of the boat to look at her. Nori's mom upends, squeaks and clicks, bobs her head, turns, and tries to get them to follow. They cut the engine and one of the big humans gets ready to drop anchor. Nori's mom returns and circles the boat, then heads for the beach where Nori lies. The humans watch her.

Nori's mom comes back again and makes tighter circles around the boat.

"I think she's trying to get us to follow her."

Someone starts the engine.

✳ ✳ ✳ ✳ ✳ ✳

People from the boat wet their towels and cover Nori. They form a line and pass buckets of water to pour over her. One of the women sits in the water near Nori's head and speaks softly to her. She has a nice voice. Offshore, Nori's mother swims back and forth. Her clicks and whistles are comforting, too.

Other boats arrive, some to watch, others to help.

"Shouldn't we drag her into deeper water?"

"No, she's sick. We've called a marine mammal rescue group. They're on the way. It's important to keep her wet and protect her from the sun."

The tide turns and is coming in again before a larger,

faster boat arrives. It, too, is full of strangers. Nori's mother swims closer.

These people unload equipment: poles and a canvas sling. The woman stroking Nori's head gets up to make room. One of them puts a disk against Nori's chest to listen to her heart, and presses his hand to her side. When he takes it away his handprint is a dent in her side.

"That's not good. She's severely dehydrated." He turns to a woman on the boat. "We'll need to hydrate her on the way in."

They remove the cool, wet towels, and spread white grease on her back.

"She's awfully thin," says the one who listened to her heart. "We're finding too many of them like this since the oil spill."

"Where will you take her?" someone asks.

"The Bayside Oceanarium in Miami. We've called, and one of our volunteers is waiting in Panama City with a plane to fly her over."

"Aren't they just an entertainment facility?"

"They also do rehabilitation." He stands. "We'll need some help here."

People line up, roll Nori to one side, and stuff the edge of the canvas sling beneath her. They roll her in the opposite direction far enough into the sling to drag her into deeper water where they can float her to the center.

Nori's frightened, and she clicks frantically for her mother as they lift her out of the water into the boat. Her mother swims back and forth just feet away.

The boat engine fires up, drowning out Nori's mother's clicks and whistles. When the boat begins to move, her mother swims alongside for as long as she can, until the throttle is shoved forward, and the bow lifts out of the water. Her mother races to keep up, but Nori's final sight of her is when she sails out of the water in the wake of the speeding boat.

"Poor thing," someone says. "It's all right, little dolphin. They'll make you better and we'll bring you back to her."

CHAPTER 10

Miami, Florida

Don's already left for a surgery and I'm feeding Adam when Suzanne calls to say she's running late, which means I'll get to school after the first-period bell—again. I hate walking into class after the teacher calls roll and having all eyes follow me to my desk.

It's always best to feed Adam before dressing him, and I should have waited to get dressed myself. I put him in his play yard and leave the oatmeal mess on the walls for Suzanne to wipe down.

She's still not there when I come out of the bathroom in a clean shirt, and my hair wet where I rinsed out the oatmeal.

I've thought for a long time that Adam knows when I'm stressed and on the verge of losing it, but I can't decide if he's upset because I'm upset—like he seemed to be with the sea lion—or takes perverse pleasure in making a bad day worse.

I give him one of his dolphins to play with, but he whacks me in the head with it and one of the flippers hits my right eye. With that eye closed against the sting, I manage to get his kicking feet through the leg holes of his Tranquility pull-on diaper, but I don't get it pulled up before he pees a stream like a water fountain, soaking the shirt I just put on. I swear he looks pleased with himself. Tears form, but I don't cry. I refuse to cry.

He screams like I'm killing him, but I finally get a T-shirt on him without dislocating one of his shoulders, put him back in his play yard, and go to my room to change clothes. My eye is still bright red and tears clump my bottom lashes together. By the clock on my nightstand, the bell will ring in twelve minutes. If Suzanne pulls in right this second and I run, I might still make it in time.

Adam is shrieking, so I get his *Little Dolphin* board book and start reading, hoping he'll stop the racket before Suzanne gets here. It's still hard to believe she's lasted nearly a month already.

I hear the gate clank open. I slam the book shut and run to the back door. "Sorry, toots," Suzanne shouts as I run past her car and out the gate before it swings closed again. School is four blocks away, but there are only five minutes left before the bell.

By block two, I'm winded and sweating and have to stop. I rest with my hands on my knees, but I'm close enough to hear the warning bell ring. One minute to the final bell and I'll have my third tardy this month, which means my third detention spent sitting in an empty classroom for an hour after school.

The security guard at the entrance looks at his watch as I trot by, but doesn't say anything. It's none of his business what time I get to school. He's supposed to be watching for lunatics with guns.

Our lockers line the breezeway wall. I'm getting my books out when the final bell rings. Instead of walking into class late, I sit on the concrete bench opposite the lockers and try to decide whether to go to class and take the detention, or skip all my classes and see what happens. I'm sure the school will call Don, but so what.

I'm sick of my day-to-day life—the morning race to get myself ready for school so I can take care of Adam until Suzanne arrives. The reverse in the afternoon: running home to relieve her by four. I'm tired of all the rushing back and forth. I'd like to sleep in one morning, and make some friends to hang out with in the afternoons, or maybe try out for soccer, or the swim team. I sit on the cool concrete bench and try to remember what life was like before Adam was born, and before Mom died. What my dreams were.

Until she met and married Don, Mom used to try to keep my father alive in my memory. Before the war, he was a marine biologist on Key Biscayne. He studied coral reefs, but was in the Navy Reserve. That's how he ended up going to Iraq. For a long time I wanted to be a marine biologist, too. I used to catch minnows in the lake in front of Baptist Hospital and keep them in a fishbowl in my room. After Mom married Don and we moved into his coral rock house, I used to inspect the outside walls with a magnifying glass and pry interesting fossil shells loose—until Don caught me. I don't know whether I outgrew wanting to be like my dad, or whether all that got buried by Adam's needs. Until this morning, I'd pretty much stopped thinking about it.

What I'd like to do right now is cross Bayshore Drive and spend the day in the park down the street, but the entire school property is fenced. The only way out is past the security guard, and he'll want to know where I'm going. Without a permission slip to leave campus, he'll call the office. I'm trapped here.

A car pulls up. Alicia hops out and slams the door. Alicia is the girl who came over to swim that time—the one who called my brother a retard.

"Hey, Lily."

"Hi."

"Whatcha doing out here?"

I press my hand to my stomach. "Got cramps. I'm waiting for a ride home."

She turns, but her mother has already pulled away. "Want me to flag Mom down? She could take you home."

"No. Our nanny's already on her way. Why are you late?"

"Dentist." She draws her lips back in a grimace to show me her braces, then peers at my hair and curls her lip. "What's that?"

I touch my head. *Oatmeal.* "I don't know."

"Looks like bird poop."

I shrug.

"How's your brother?" She smiles, and I hate her all over again. "Better run," she says. "See ya."

I go to the girls' bathroom and wash the oatmeal out of my hair and then go back and sit with my back against one of the posts holding up the breezeway roof. I read until first period ends and kids boil out of classrooms.

When the second period starts, I gather my stuff and head for the library.

The library is in the southwest corner of the school. I find an overstuffed chair opposite the row of windows facing a side street. From this seat, I have a nice view of the trees and can look up from my book to watch the palm fronds dipping and swaying in the breeze. The silent movement of the fronds makes me feel deaf. I'm thinking I'd rather be deaf than blind when two girls walk past the window. They are giggling and looking back over their shoulders. One of them glances my way, but, for whatever reason, doesn't see me. Maybe the windows mirror the trees, so she can't see me watching. It's a familiar feeling—invisibility.

After second period ends, I go to lunch with the third-period kids and fix myself a salad from the salad bar. When I turn, I see a girl who's in my language arts class sitting by herself at one end of a long table. She glances at me and kind of smiles. I pretend not to notice and take my tray to an empty table in the corner. Sometimes I feel sorry for myself that I don't have any friends, but the fact that I don't is my own fault. I prefer being alone to acquiring another Alicia. Our school is very strict about bullying, or I would probably be bullied. Instead, I'm ignored, which suits me fine.

When the cafeteria starts to empty out, I hide in the girls' bathroom until the fourth-period bell rings. I follow them into the cafeteria and have a bowl of soup this time. When fifth period comes in for lunch, I have a ham-and-cheese sandwich.

I keep thinking any minute someone is going to notice that I've eaten three lunches and have been hanging out most of the day, but no one does.

For sixth period, I go back in the library, find my corner unoccupied, and read until school lets out at three thirty, when I leave for home, satisfied with my day.

* * * * * *

The automated message on the answering machine says, "Your child missed one or more classes today. Please call the office at your earliest convenience." I delete it seconds before Don comes into the kitchen.

"How was school?"

Of course, I think, he knows. "Why?" My tone is defensive in spite of the fact my heart is now lodged in my throat.

He lifts an eyebrow, and I think he's going to threaten me with . . . with what? He can't ground me. I never go anywhere. What can he do? Send me to my room without dinner? I had three nice lunches.

He shrugs, and I realize he asks me most days how school went, I say fine, and our dance ends. My guilty conscience made me jump to the wrong conclusion.

Don pours himself a glass of orange juice and walks to the window that looks out at the pool. "Did the yard-man come today?"

"How should I know? I was at school, remember?"

He turns. "Doesn't look like he did," he says, like it's my fault. "What are you smiling about?"

"I'm not." But I was. Don always finds a way around what he considers an obstacle to getting what he wants. I'm smiling because I can be a rule breaker, too.

He puts his empty glass beside the sink, leaves the orange juice carton on the counter—for me to put away, I guess—and goes outside, probably to measure the height of the grass.

CHAPTER 11

I don't know if the school bothered to call Don again. If they did, he never confronted me, so on the following Tuesday, when Suzanne is late again, I don't make the same mistake. After she arrives, I dart down the driveway like I'm racing to get to school, but as soon as the gate closes, I turn right and leisurely drift the four blocks to Kennedy Park.

Sweaty joggers circle the vita course, stopping at exercise stations. A carload of boys honks and laughs at a bunch of old people in a tai chi class doing slow-motion kung fu moves. I walk straight down to the bay. The water is murky and full of trash—plastic ice bags, Styrofoam cups, other bits of unidentifiable plastic. People are pigs.

It's hot and still, but later, when the breeze picks up, there will be sailboats to watch. I look around for a shady place to sit where I can read. The only bench facing the water is occupied by a sleeping homeless man. He's covered himself from head to ankles with sheets of the *Miami Herald*. His boots, with the upper parts separated from the soles, expose filthy toes, which are pointed skyward. Every once in a while he shakes a foot to rid it of flies.

Now that I'm here, I wonder what I'm going to do all day. I've got a book, but I'll be done reading it in a couple of hours. I think about walking to the Grove and wandering the shops, maybe see a movie, but nothing's open yet.

I decide to go watch the tai chi class and walk back toward Bayshore Drive where the morning traffic, headed for downtown, is bumper-to-bumper. I take a bench facing the old people.

There's nothing unusual about people honking at each other in Miami traffic, but I do look up when I hear a guy shout, "All clear, girly." Some of the people in the tai chi class also pause to look.

Traffic has stopped in both directions to let a girl cross the street. People in Miami never stop for pedestrians, except maybe in school zones. One car, driven by a man talking on his cell phone, pulls forward to plug the gap left by the car in front of him and moves into the path of the girl. I see him jump, like maybe she whacked the side of his car. His window goes down. I can't hear what they say, but she nods, turns to her left, and walks around the front of his car. That's when I see the white cane. A moment later, she taps the curb, steps up, and crosses the parking lot without her cane hitting a single car, even though the lot is nearly full.

The jogging path is made of tightly packed wood chips and feels spongy underfoot. She crosses the grass, finds the edge of the path with her cane, steps to the center, tucks her cane into the crook of her arm, and walks it like a sighted person.

I get up and follow her, staying on the grass so she won't hear me.

As we get closer to the water, a breeze kicks up. The blind girl stops, lifts her chin, and takes a deep breath. If occurs to me that, till now, she has been walking through thick, humid silence. I wonder, when there are no sounds, if it's like moving through nothingness. Hearing the palm fronds rattle and leaves rustle must furnish the landscape for her. I'm reminded of sitting in the library last week when I cut classes, watching tree branches moving in the wind and deciding I'd rather be deaf than blind.

To get to the bay, she has to either continue on the path, which circles the entire park, or cross the grass and dodge the trees. If it was me, I'd stick to the path, but she uses her cane to find where the lawn starts and, with her nose held high, heads straight for the water. Maybe she's planning to drown herself. I might if I was blind. This gives me a good excuse to stick close. If she wades in and goes under, I'll be there to sound the alarm, and jump in to save her.

Instead of swinging her cane widely from side to side, she's sweeping it in a narrow arc just ahead of where she's stepping. I move around to get in front of her and realize she's making a soft clicking sound with her tongue—like water dripping. I'm tempted to warn her she's headed for a tree, but something about the sureness of her pace makes me think she knows it's there. When she's a yard or two away, she tucks the cane into the crook of her arm and keeps walking. The clicking turns to humming, and she begins turning her head from side to side. Two feet short of the tree, she reaches out, touches the trunk with her fingers, and runs her hand over the bark. "Gumbo limbo," she says, and turns back toward the bay.

I walk over to the tree, close my eyes, and feel the trunk. The bark on gumbo limbo trees peels in sheets, leaving the deep maroon-colored trunk smooth and cool to the touch. Locals call them tourist trees because the thin, papery bark looks like sheets of skin hanging off sunburned Yankees.

I trot after her. She's using her cane again but hasn't stopped humming or clicking, or moving her head. She reminds me of an owl homing in on a mouse. There are trees on both sides of the route she's taking, the largest of which is to her left. When she tucks her cane and veers straight for it, I decide she's only pretending to be blind— until she bumps into a metal mesh trash can. She feels the rim of it, gives a little laugh, steps around it, and begins to hum again. A few feet short of running right into the tree, she reaches out and touches the trunk. It's a ficus tree, but she's having trouble figuring that out since there are usually masses of thin roots hanging from the branches. This one's been trimmed. The aerial roots are starting to grow back but dangle from branches way above her head. She circles the tree, swinging her cane until she finds a branch with leaves low enough for her to reach. She feels a leaf and smiles. "Ficus."

While trying to find a low branch, she ends up facing back the way she came. Her chin goes up and she sniffs the air, turns, and starts for the bay again.

I fall in behind her and watch her check out every tree on her way to the water. Most are Australian pines; the last is a sea grape growing at the water's edge. She stands near it and breathes deeply, then, using her cane, she heads for the park bench where the homeless man is now sitting up.

This is my first good look at her face. She's my age, pretty with long, straight black hair; kind of Native American–looking with high cheekbones. She's not wearing dark glasses like other blind people, and I can see her clear brown eyes. Again, it occurs to me that she may be pretending, though she's staring straight ahead and doesn't blink.

She stops short of the bench, as if she's seen the homeless man. He's been watching her, too.

"I'd like to sit there if you don't mind sharing."

The guy glances over his shoulder and sees me. "I was leaving." He stands unsteadily, leans to gather up the newspaper, and almost falls over. "You want I should leave the paper?"

I gasp at his rudeness, and the girl turns in my direction. She smiles and faces him again. He isn't exactly where she's looking anymore. He's stepped to one side. "Is it the Braille edition?"

"Ha. That's a good one. I was blind myself last night."

When he says that, she adjusts where she's looking to where he's standing. "Do you have insight this morning, or just sight?"

It takes him a moment to interpret this, and he laughs. "Same as every morning: I can see, but ain't too interested in keeping my eyes open for long."

I'm thinking, *How can you say that to a blind person?* when the girl steps forward and puts her hand out. It's about six inches to the right of where he's standing, but he reaches for it, pulls his hand back, wipes it on his dirty pants, and shakes her hand.

"My name is Zoe."

"I'm Dwayne."

"Nice to meet you, Dwayne."

"Wouldn't be if you could see me."

"I don't agree. I see differently, but quite clearly."

"Ain't you blind?"

"I am, but that means I only see what's important about a person, not their physical self."

"Like if you was God and I was dead?"

Zoe smiles. "A little like that."

"Can I help you to the bench?" Dwayne says.

"No need. I do okay, considering."

"I'd like to anyway." He steps forward and takes her arm. "I'm here most mornings, if I don't get run off by a cop the night before. Maybe I'll see you again."

"I hope so."

He leaves Zoe on the bench facing the water, but not

before he stacks the newspapers, brushes off the seat, and picks at a dried spot of bird poop with his index finger.

"Thanks, Dwayne."

"You're welcome, missy."

I'm standing with my arms at my sides. I miss my mother more at this moment than in the nearly two years since she died, but I'm not sure why. I feel like she's holding me in place, pinning my arms to my sides, refusing to let me move, refusing to let me hide.

Dwayne glances at me. "Is that girl there a friend of yours?"

"Not yet." Zoe looks in my general direction.

Why would I want to make friends with another person with needs? I walk away. Not far. Just away.

CHAPTER 12

Dwayne leaves and I stare at the bay where the sun creates stars on the waves. I glance over at Zoe every once in a while. I could walk over and tell her how the bay looks in the sun and that way out there, almost to the horizon, a thunderhead is forming, but I don't.

She's taken a book from her backpack and is reading with her fingertips, but she's listening at the same time. A blue jay flies over, and she looks up; a jogger runs by and returns her nod of good morning, sees her white cane leaning against the bench, and says, "Good morning," out loud.

Whenever her head turns in my direction, I hold my breath. She can't see me any more than Adam can, but the difference is she wants to.

"Are you still here?" she says.

For a second I think I won't answer, but I do. "Yes."

"I'm Zoe."

"I know. I've been watching you. I'm Lily."

"Am I a peculiar sight?"

"It's not that."

"Do you know other blind people?"

"Not really."

"You must be pretty bored to spend a day like this in the park following a blind girl around."

"What makes you think I've been following you?"

"I heard you breathing." Zoe lifts her chin and sniffs. "And I like your shampoo."

"I was worried you'd run into a tree."

"Nice of you to worry, but I'm getting better at locating them." She smiles. "Thigh-high trash cans are another story."

"Is that what the humming and clicking was about?" I walk over and stand between her and the bay.

She turns to face me. "I'm practicing echolocation."

I can't figure out how she knew I'd moved until I realize I'm blocking the breeze. "Echolocation? Like a dolphin?"

"Or a bat. There's a guy who teaches the blind to navigate using echolocation. I'm not very good yet, but I'll keep trying."

"How's it supposed to work?"

"Sounds bounce off solid objects. If I hum and turn my head side to side, I can hear the subtle difference between a tree and no tree." She grins. "Or Lily and no Lily. Want to help me practice?"

"Sure."

Zoe puts her book on the bench and stands. "You'll have to come at me from downwind so I can't smell your shampoo."

I cross the path to the grass and walk about ten feet into the park. Zoe feels her way around to the back of the bench and stands facing my general direction.

"I'm ready." She starts to hum and move her head from side to side.

A step at a time, I walk toward her. For the first few feet it's clear she doesn't have a clue where I am or which direction I'm coming from. A breeze kicks up and she holds up her hand to stop me until the trees are still again.

A lady walking her dog on the vita course glances at me, then at Zoe humming and swinging her head. Zoe hears her dog's tags jingling. "Nice day."

The woman sees her cane. "It is indeed."

Zoe waits until she's gone to start humming again.

I'm a yard away when Zoe homes in on where I am.

She smiles, but goes on humming, though the width of her head turns is less. I take another step toward her. She puts her hand up, and we high-five.

"That's really cool."

"Mom says the guy who teaches echolocation takes blind people on bike rides on forest trails. I'd like to get that good." She turns back toward the bench. "May I?" She puts her hand on my shoulder.

"Sure." I lead her to the bench.

"Do you live around here?" We both speak at once and laugh.

"You first," she says.

"I live about four blocks west."

"Me, too."

"You sound my age," Zoe says. "Why aren't you in school?"

"I took a day off. Why aren't you?"

"I'm homeschooled." She smiles. "But I'll be going to Biscayne Middle School in the fall."

"That's where I go!"

"Do you skip often?"

"This is the first time." Which is kind of the truth. I change the subject. "Did you walk all the way down here by yourself?"

"Yes and no. Yes, I walked here by myself. It's not hard. I count the blocks. And no, my mother followed me. Can you see the parking lot from here?"

"Yes."

"Is there a Prius parked there?"

"There are two. Both white."

"One is Mom. If she's not sitting in it, she's somewhere around here, watching. I don't think she'll really let me walk to the park alone until I'm married."

I laugh. "Do you mind if I ask a question?"

"No."

"Why the park when you can't see how pretty it is?"

"I come here to practice echolocation, but go ahead and tell me what you see."

"Green grass, the trees, sailboats on the bay, the way the water sparkles in the sun."

Zoe smiles. "You take in what you see in a gulp. I sip. I smell the grass, which was recently mowed, and the trees have different bark, smells, and leaves. Some have flowers and seeds. I smell the bay, feel the sun, and can remember how it looks on the water. I smell the trash that's caught in the rocks at the water's edge. I hear the joggers and their iPods. But if it makes you feel better, the last time I was here, I stepped in a fire ant hill. Now I'm careful to feel for their mounds with my cane."

"What's it like when there's no sound?"

"There's always sound. The air is never empty, but I do love it when the breeze is blowing. It fills my mind with images. I use my ears to read the landscape and am always measuring and memorizing my steps." Zoe turns her head toward a bird singing.

"That's pretty," I say.

"It's a male cardinal. They're bright red. Do you see it?"

I look around until I spot the bird. "You're right. It's on the ground under the sea grape tree. Guess that doesn't help much."

"No. It does."

"I don't know birds by their songs, and only a few by sight," I say. "I had a pet Quaker parakeet once, but Mom and I set it free. How did you learn them if, you know . . . ?"

"If I can't see them?"

"Uh-huh."

"I wasn't always blind, so when something is described to me, my mind creates a picture. Because you told me where it is, I can see the male cardinal under the sea grape."

I look at Zoe's clear brown eyes. "Do you mind me asking what happened?"

"Cancer. Retinoblastoma. First one eye when I was two and the other when I was four. These"—she points to her eyes—"are prostheses. Better than two holes in my head, don't you think?"

I laugh. "Much. They look so real I thought you were pretending to be blind at first."

We sit for a few minutes looking out at the water, not saying anything.

"I probably should go," Zoe says. "I hate to waste Mom's entire day. What are you going to do?"

"Walk into town, I guess. Maybe go to a movie. I can't go home until after school is out."

Zoe gets up. "Do you have your cell with you?"

I nod, then remember she can't see me. "Yeah."

"Let me give you my number. Maybe we could go shopping one day. I love my mother, but I don't trust her taste in clothes. Maybe you'd help me pick out a few outfits for school."

"Sure, I guess. I'm free Saturday if my stepfather doesn't find out I skipped school and ground me."

As I put her number in my cell phone, "Do you swim?" pops out of my mouth.

"I do."

Before I can say another word, I see Alicia grin at me and ask how my brother's doing, but then I think of the way Zoe treated Dwayne. "We have a pool."

"Are you inviting me over?"

"I guess."

"You don't sound too enthused."

"My brother is autistic. Some people—"

"You're worried I'll be put off by his disability." She closes her eyes, holds her hands out, and waves them blindly, like she's feeling for an obstacle.

She makes me laugh again, and it feels good.

CHAPTER 13

Suzanne's at the sink when I come in from the movie a little before four. She turns and puts her finger to her lips. "Adam's asleep."

I close the back door quietly and tiptoe to the refrigerator for the orange juice and take a glass from the drain board.

Suzanne nods toward the den. "Don's home and on the warpath."

My heart jumps. "I didn't see his car."

"It's in for an oil change. Someone from the shop gave him a ride home." Suzanne opens her arms and I walk into them. "It will be okay, toots. Let him blow his top, promise never to do it again, and forget about it."

Suzanne suddenly lets me go, and I turn. Don is standing on the other side of the center island. "In my office. Now."

"If you wake Adam after the day I've had, I'll quit." Suzanne's hands are on her hips. "Take it outside."

Don's who-do-you-think-you're-talking-to look deflates. He points a stiff arm and forefinger at the back door.

I walk and he follows. "What were you thinking?" he says before he closes the door.

Suzanne jerks the doorknob out of his hand. "All the way out!"

Don grabs my arm and marches me across the patio, out into the yard, and turns me to face him.

"Where were you?"

"In the park for a while, then I went to a movie." Being so matter-of-fact about it seems to throw him.

"Why?"

I shrug. "I needed a day for myself."

"You don't think I could use a day off? You have responsibilities. One is school, and the other is to help with your brother."

"Help with him, or raise him for you?"

I can't believe I said that, and I feel like I can't breathe.

For a second, Don looks punched in the gut, then he balls his fists. I take a breath and go on. "I wasn't late coming home."

"That's not the point."

"What is, then? I'm always here for him, and I

shouldn't have to be. I'm not Momma." My voice cracks. "I'm his twelve-year-old sister. Remember?"

"You're grounded."

I actually laugh. "What does that mean?" I'm facing the house and can see Suzanne watching from the kitchen. Knowing she's on my side, or at least understands, makes me braver. "I can't go out with friends, can't go to the mall, can't watch TV. How do you see this grounding thing?"

"Don't sass me, young lady. What would your mother say?"

No fair. I glance again at the window. Suzanne's not there. No one is there. I hear Adam wailing.

Don sighs. "There are going to be some new rules around here."

"No, there aren't. I'm a good kid; I make good grades; I miss . . ." Tears well. "I miss my mother." Sweat runs down the side of my face and from my underarms.

"Then just think about how disappointed she'd be in your behavior."

There's no escape. I think about screaming, like Adam. Throw myself to the ground, kick my feet in the air, and shriek at the top of my lungs.

"Your attitude lately . . ." He drones on, but I stop listening until he says, "We're going to make some changes."

"Good," I say. "You can start by getting help for Adam. Take him back to the Cutler Academy or find a dolphin therapy program. Something." I run across the yard and dive into the pool, swim the length under water, and come up at the shallow end. Don's standing at the deep end.

I turn to face him. "I made a friend today in the park, and she's coming over Saturday to go swimming."

"You need to watch Adam on Saturday. It's Suzanne's day off, and I have rounds in the morning."

"I'll watch him in the morning. When you finish rounds, you can take over."

Suzanne comes out the back door leading Adam, who's covered in poop, by the hand. "You should see the walls in his room."

I get out of the pool, uncoil the garden hose, hand it to Don, and dive back in the pool, where I let myself drift down until I settle on the bottom. I watch the blurry dance they're doing—Don holding both of Adam's wrists clamped in one fist; Adam's toes brushing the grass, trying to touch the ground and run; Suzanne washing him down. I stay until I run out of air and have to shoot to the surface.

I come out of my room after changing into dry clothes. Adam's dolphin video is on and he's in his high chair, flapping his hands and squeaking at the screen. Don is talking to Suzanne in the kitchen.

"I'm not the answer. You have to get qualified help for your son."

I back up before they see me and pin myself to the wall.

"Lily needs some semblance of a childhood. She's wonderful with *your* son—" I love the emphasis on *your*. "But she needs some space."

I go back into my room and sit at my desk. I'm feeling sorry for myself, but the doll head shows no emotion at all. I turn it to face the wall, find my cell phone, and call Zoe. Her mother answers.

"This is Lily Moran. May—"

"Hello, Lily. Zoe told me about meeting you. I'll get her."

I hear her mother call, then silence. I think about that. In this house, there is never silence.

"Hi, Lily."

"Hi. Would you like—"

"I'd love to. Saturday?"

I laugh. "Yeah. Don's got rounds until after lunch, so I'll walk over to get you around one."

"Mom'll drop me off." Zoe lowers her voice. "She wants to know where I'll be. But you can walk me home."

* * * * * *

After dinner of pizza and a store-bought salad, I start Adam's dolphin DVD again and go to my room. I stand with my back to the window, judge the distance to my door, then kick my wet shorts and T-shirt out of the way so the path is clear. I close my eyes, begin to hum and walk toward it, but after a few feet, I'm not so sure of the distance any longer. I should open the door so I'm walking toward an open space, not solid walls, but I don't want Don to catch me. If echolocation works, I should know when I'm getting close. I hum and turn my head side to side like Zoe did, but it doesn't work and I have to put my hands out until I touch the wall.

I creep down the hall, through the laundry room, and out the door to the pool. There's a birdbath full of dead leaves in the far corner of the yard. I focus on it, close my eyes, and start across the grass. A breeze stirs the palms. I stop to listen, go about ten more feet before I get the urge to peek. I know there's nothing between me and the birdbath except a few sprinkler heads. I put my hands out to protect myself in case I trip and fall. I wonder if this is what Zoe goes through—feeling her way through life, every step an uncertainty. I don't think so. Even with my eyes open, my life is more uncertain than hers.

CHAPTER 14

Don has left this morning's *Miami Herald* on the kitchen counter, folded to a story about a young dolphin flown from the Gulf of Mexico to the Bayside Oceanarium on Key Biscayne.

Hope Fades for Young Dolphin with Cancer

Nori, the young coastal bottlenose dolphin rescued near Panama City ten days ago, is showing little improvement since being airlifted to Bayside Oceanarium. Nori and her mother were part of an AquaPlanet summer program for handicapped and autistic children who come to swim with wild dolphins in the warm waters off Panama City.

More than 650 dolphins have been found stranded in the spill area since the

Gulf oil disaster began. This is more than four times the historic average. The National Oceanic and Atmospheric Administration calls it an "Unusual Mortality Event." Most, by the time they are found, are severely ill and showing signs of liver and lung disease—all symptoms consistent with those seen in other mammals exposed to oil.

This young dolphin was diagnosed with a malignant lesion under her tongue. The tumor was successfully removed, but the Oceanarium's veterinarians aren't sure why the young dolphin isn't responding to efforts to save her.

Over the top of the paper, I see Adam sitting on the floor of his play yard, making the sign for eat. He stands and begins to jerk on a side panel, trying to get out.

Don's in his office.

"Did you feed Adam?"

"Not yet. He just woke up."

I bet. I put the paper down and get the egg carton

from the fridge. "Why'd you leave me a sad story about a dying dolphin?"

At the word *dolphin*, Adam starts to squeak.

Don gets up and comes to the kitchen. "I've been asked to come take a look at her. I thought maybe we'd go out Saturday after my rounds at the hospital."

"Why'd they ask you?"

"Cancer's my specialty. I think the vet wants to be assured he's done all he can. I said yes because it might end up giving Adam another opportunity to swim with dolphins."

"Do they have a therapy program?"

"They used to." He smiles. "Maybe they will again."

"I've invited Zoe over to swim."

"Zoe?"

"The girl I met in the . . ." I hesitate. I don't really want to remind Don that I skipped school. "You remember, I told you about her."

He shrugs. "Bring her with us."

"Really?"

"Sure. Why not?"

I turn to the stove, grinning. Don has been nicer to me since Suzanne talked to him. "Did you eat?"

"I had toast."

"Want an egg?"

"Sure. Thanks." He goes back to his office, sits, and turns in his chair so he can see me. "Another thing. Adam starts at the Cutler Academy on Monday."

Wow. "Why'd you change your mind?" I open the pantry door so Don can't see me and pump the air with my fist.

"I was too rash," he says.

I'm glad he can't see me roll my eyes.

"It can't hurt to give it a try."

I close the pantry door and break another egg into the glass bowl, add a little milk, and start to beat them. Adam puts his hands over his ears and screams.

"Now what?" Don shouts.

"I don't know," I say, though I'm sure it was the sharp sound of the fork hitting the glass bowl that set him off.

I lift Adam out of his play yard to put him in his high chair, but he squirms out of my arms, dodges past me, runs down the hall, and disappears into his room.

When I catch up, he's tearing through the toy box. I stand in the doorway, watching. The more frustrated he gets not to find whatever he's looking for, the louder he shrieks. I close the door behind me so he can't get out, and sink to the floor.

He gets quiet and smiles. Not at me, but at the book in his hands. It's his *Little Dolphin* finger puppet book.

He brings it to me, turns, and sits his butt in my lap with his back to my chest. I put my finger in the puppet and open the first page. The book is showing the wear of having been read a million times. I start on the first page.

"'Little Dolphin wants to play . . . but where are all his friends today?'"

I wiggle the puppet and turn the page. My heart is not in this. It brings back too many memories of Mom, the dolphins at Ocean Reef, and us as a family before Adam showed the signs of autism.

"'Someone must have heard his call! Here comes a friend. They'll have a ball!'"

Adam flaps his fingers against his palm—his version of dolphins swimming, I guess—and squeaks.

The next two pages are sticky. I pry them apart with my fingernail.

"'While splashing and swimming and spinning around, they talk to each other with dolphin sounds.'"

Pages seven and eight are stuck together, so I skip them.

"'But in the light of the setting sun . . .'"

Adam screams and kicks his legs.

"What?"

He grabs the book and tries to pull apart the pages that are stuck together.

"Gimme that. You're going to ruin it." I pry his fingers loose and hold the book up out of his reach. "Let me do it." I stand and open the door. Adam, shrieking, follows me down the hall and across the living room to the kitchen. He falls to the floor and kicks at my legs while I use a steak knife to pry the stuck pages apart.

Once I've fixed it, I sit beside him and put my finger in the puppet. "Hush, or I'm not going to read to you."

He quiets, sits up, then crawls into my lap and presses his back to my chest. I go to the pages I pried apart.

"'They take turns leaping through the air, like acrobats, they make a pair.'"

Adam flaps his fingers.

"'But in the light of the setting sun, the friends must end their day of fun.'"

Adam giggles.

"'Little Dolphin swims home through the deep, looking forward to peaceful sleep. Sleep tight, Little Dolphin!'" I lean and kiss Adam's cheek, then look up. Don is standing over us.

"Remember this book?"

He nods.

"Two pages were stuck together and Adam made a fuss when I skipped them."

"He probably saw that you skipped them."

"He wasn't looking at the book. He was flapping his fingers."

"Your mother read that book to him a thousand times. He's probably got it memorized."

"That was nearly half his life ago."

Don shrugs.

Adam grabs the book from me, closes it, and hands it back, then begins to flap his fingers against his palm.

Don says, "You're no longer in danger of getting suspended."

"Was I?"

"Yes, you certainly were. But I told the school you missed because I had an emergency and you were taking care of your brother."

I try not to show my surprise.

"And I told them you're going to have to miss Monday, too."

"I am?"

"Don't you want to be there for Adam's first day of school?"

"Sure," I say, but am pretty sure the real reason Don wants me there is he needs me to help handle Adam.

CHAPTER 15

Saturday noon, and Don's still not home from the hospital when I hear the buzzer for the driveway gate. I look at the camera and see Zoe in the front seat of her mother's white Prius. I press the intercom. "Hi, Zoe. The code is 0514."

Her mother lowers her window and punches in Don's birth date.

After Zoe introduces me to her mom, I tell them about the sick dolphin and ask her mother if it's okay for Zoe to go with us to the Oceanarium.

"It's sad about the little dolphin, but I think the Oceanarium sounds fun. Call if you're going to be late." She pats Zoe's cheek.

Like she did in the park, Zoe says, "May I?" and holds up her left hand.

"Sure." I turn my back and lean toward her until her fingertips touch my right shoulder, then I lead her to the back door, remembering to warn her about the step up into the laundry room.

Adam is in his play yard, lining up his stuffed dolphins from small to large. He's been squeaking to them, but for these few moments the house is quiet.

I lead Zoe to the kitchen's center aisle, and pull a stool out for her. "I was fixing Adam lunch. Are you hungry?"

"I ate, thanks. Where is he?" Her head is cocked, listening for him.

"He's over there in his play yard with his stuffed dolphins."

Zoe smiles.

"Sorry," I say, remembering that *over there* means nothing to her. "He's in the living room, which is on your left. He's been quiet for almost a full minute. I don't expect it to last."

"I read up on autism online."

I blurt. "How?"

"I have JAWS on my computer." She smiles, then clacks her teeth together. "It's a text-to-speech software."

"Someone reads everything to you? That's cool."

Zoe smiles again, and I realize how little I understand what it's like to be blind.

"How old was Adam when he was diagnosed?"

"Two, but Mom thought there was something wrong a year before that."

"My mom was hoping to meet your mother. Is she home?"

A lump forms in my throat, and I shake my head.

"Lily?" She turns her head, thinking, I suppose, that I've moved or left the kitchen without her hearing me.

"My mother's dead. She was killed in a car accident two years ago."

Zoe gets up and follows the edge of the counter around to where I'm standing. She puts her arms around me. "I'm so sorry."

I don't want her to hug me, and stiffen. She lets go and steps back.

"I'm a touchy-feely kind of person, obviously."

"It's not that. I don't want people feeling sorry for me."

"I know what you mean." She smiles, and with one hand following the edge of the counter, goes back to her stool.

"I guess I feel sorry enough for myself without help from anyone else." I get Adam's divided plate from the drain board, put applesauce in one section, carrot sticks in another, and bite-sized cubes of chicken in the third.

Zoe's head is tilted like she hears something. "I think your dad's home."

"He's my stepfather."

The back door opens and Don walks in. Zoe turns and smiles at him. "Hello, Dr. Moran. I'm Zoe." She puts her hand out—a little to the left of where he's standing.

Don looks at her hand, then at those pretty fake eyes, then at the white cane leaning against the counter. "You're . . . you're—"

"Blind." She laughs.

I want to kick him in the shins.

"Lily didn't tell me."

"That's good," Zoe says. "It means it wasn't that important to her."

Don steps forward and takes her hand. "It's nice to meet you," he says, then crooks a finger at me. "May I speak to you in my office?"

I follow him across the living room, and he closes the door behind us. "She's blind."

"So?"

"I need you to take care of Adam while we're there. How can you watch him and lead her around at the same time? And if she can't see anything, how is she going to enjoy herself?"

"Zoe doesn't need to be led around. You'll be amazed at what she 'sees.'" I make quotations marks with my fingers.

"I don't think so. Go out there and tell her some other time, and that we'll drop her home on our way."

"I've invited her and she's going." My hand is on the doorknob when I turn to look at him. "Or we both stay here and you and Adam can go."

"What has gotten into you?" he snaps.

I shrug. *A spine?* Or maybe it's because I don't feel so alone with Suzanne willing to speak up for me. Still, I'm not quite brave enough to say *a spine* out loud.

Zoe has located Adam and is sitting on the floor by his play yard. He's not looking at her, but he knows she's there. He's squeaking and holding one of his dolphins in her direction.

Zoe copies the sound and Adam goes silent.

"You and I can talk to dolphins. That's a special gift."

Don is standing behind me. I hear him breathing.

Adam scrambles his neat line of dolphins with his feet, then throws his dolphin finger puppet book over the side of the play yard. It lands with a thud a few inches from Zoe's right knee. She reaches and picks it up.

I turn and grin at Don, then realize Zoe won't be able to read it to him, which may set Adam off.

Zoe feels the cover and finds the puppet. "This is one of the finger puppet books. I had them all when I was little." She feels the puppet. "It doesn't have ears, so it must be *Little Dolphin*." She looks up and smiles in our direction, which means she knows we're there watching.

Zoe wiggles the puppet and squeaks, and Adam, without looking at her, holds up one of his dolphins and squeaks back at her.

That's the second time in three weeks that he's done something in response to something someone said. Debra and now Zoe. I give Don a see-I-told-you-so look.

"I like your friend," he whispers next to my ear.

Zoe hears like an owl, and I see a hint of a smile on her lips. "Good, Adam. That's exactly how dolphins talk to each other."

I'm sorry Zoe felt she had to win Don over, but I'm glad she did.

CHAPTER 16

The main parking lot of the Oceanarium is half full, but there's a line of cars to pay the parking fee.

"Eight dollars," the parking attendant says when it's our turn.

"Dr. Moran," Don says.

The guy stares at him blankly.

"Dr. Moran," Don says again. "I'm expected."

The parking guy steps into his booth and picks up the phone. He turns his back when someone answers, but I still hear him say, "Well, nobody told *me*."

He tears a blue ticket in half and hands it to Don through the window.

A high school–aged kid waits for us at the gate to a rear entrance. He's fumbling with a set of keys when we pull up and keeps glancing over his shoulder at Don, who isn't helping by drumming the steering wheel with his fingers. When he finally gets the gate open, Don drives through and nods thanks.

We park near four round concrete tanks, all of which are painted blue. Three of them are nearly ground level and look like they might have once been a sewage treatment plant. One is full of green algae; two are empty except for puddles of rainwater, pine needles, and pollen.

The fourth has walls higher than Adam is tall so he can't see the dolphin inside. She's floating on the surface near a raft chained to two rusty metal rings embedded in the wall. The dolphin rolls to look at us, but is otherwise listless.

I can see Biscayne Bay through a gap in the Australian pines that line the shore, and behind us is the gold dome of the Oceanarium. I came here once on a field trip a couple of years before Mom died. I don't think Mom liked this place, but I remember having fun.

The Oceanarium's vet comes along a path from the opposite direction and joins us at the railing around the tank. He's carrying a medical chart, nods at me and Zoe, and shakes Don's hand. "Nice of you to come."

"Not at all. The kids are excited."

When Don says that, the vet actually looks at us for the first time. Unlike Don, who has honed his bedside-manner skills so his face is nearly always a mask, the vet's expression hides nothing. He sees Zoe's cane and studies her eyes. I can see his mind working. How can she be blind with such perfect-looking eyes? Then I see it dawn on him that they're not real. His gaze switches to Adam, straining against his Kid Keeper harness, the top of his diaper showing above the waistband of his pants, then to me. I bore him. He turns sideways to stand beside Don, and flips open the chart.

"As I told you on the phone, it was a squamous cell carcinoma large enough to deviate the tongue to the left. The mass was removed in a series of five sections until we got clean margins. Postoperatively, she did very well. She received 100 mg carprofen IM after the procedure—"

Zoe interrupts. "What does IM mean?" Which is what I wanted to know, but never would have asked.

"Intramuscular," Don says. "Into the muscle."

The vet studies Zoe again, and goes on. "Follow-up has included flushing the wound with a fifty percent vinegar solution and monitoring for any recurrence at the incision line."

"Any indication of metastases?"

"None, but I'd still like you to look at her X-rays. The lungs and abdomen appear clear and the mass did not infiltrate the mandible. The surgical wound healed, and we've kept her on antibiotics, but she's not improving."

Somewhere, on the other side of a high wall, a loud-speaker announces the next dolphin show will start in ten minutes in the upper deck tank. Adam hears *dolphin* and starts to squeal.

"He loves d-o-l-p-h-i-n-s," Don says, and gives me a warning glance, like I could possibly stop Adam from throwing a tantrum if he thinks there's a dolphin here and we're keeping him from it.

Zoe listened to what the vet said, then left us. She's walking the circumference of the tank, the diameter of which is about twenty-five feet. Our swimming pool is much longer than this tank is wide. Zoe leans over like she's watching the dolphin, but I hear her humming and clicking softly. The dolphin drifts over and rolls to look at her.

"That poor thing has got to be dying of boredom," Zoe whispers to me when she comes back to where we're standing. Her right hand is a mass of tiny blue paint chips that came off as she guided herself around the tank.

Don gives me the dirty look that would be wasted on Zoe, but his expression goes blank when Zoe turns to where he and the vet are standing. Maybe she heard him mentally snarling.

"They communicate with sonar, you know," Zoe says, louder now. "If she tries to use it in that tank, the sound bounces off the concrete. There's nothing for her to see, no picture for her to create in her mind except wall, wall, wall."

I glance at the vet and then at Don.

"I'm sure they have her isolated for a purpose." Don's voice is flat.

"This is the tank we had free." The vet's tone is defensive.

Zoe homes in on where the vet's standing and walks over. "Imagine yourself recovering from an illness completely isolated, sealed into a concrete container. She might as well be in the bottom of a well. She can see walls and the sky and nothing else."

Don gives me a threatening look.

"She's cut off from the world." Zoe's tone is so full of passion that I think this is as much about her as it is about the dolphin.

Don clears his throat in a way that suggests his tolerance for her interruptions is at an end.

Since Zoe can't see people's faces, she can't know

when to shut up. "What's her name, again?" I say, hoping Zoe will take the hint and hush.

The vet flips the pages of her chart until he finds the answer. "Her name is Nori."

Zoe leans over the wall, calls her name, and lets out a series of whistles and clicks.

Adam begins to hop up and down, flap his fingers against his palm, and squeak.

Nori upends and blows a long call through her blowhole.

Adam tries to scale the wall of the tank. I catch him and lift him so he can see Nori. I have one arm around his waist and am holding tight to the straps of his harness with my right hand. Adam swings his arms and starts kicking his feet. If I dropped him in the tank, he'd be swimming.

"Your son really does like dolphins," the vet says. "I don't see any harm in letting him get on the raft to pet her. Maybe he's just what she needs."

Don doesn't hesitate. "That's nice of you." He says to me, "You go down first and I'll lower Adam to you."

I look at Zoe, then at Don. He shakes his head, then reconsiders. Better to have her down there than up here bugging the vet. "Zoe, would you like to go, too?"

"Oh, yes." She heads straight for the ladder, the steps of which her cane hit when she first circled the tank.

She feels the railing and counts the steps, then leans her cane against the wall, climbs up the side of the tank, and starts down the other side. I tell her when she's reached the last step. The raft is wobbly, so I wait until she's on it and lying on her stomach before I start down the ladder.

Zoe makes clicking sounds.

"She's on the far side of the tank, watching you."

"Come here, Nori." Zoe stirs the water with her hand.

Nori makes a sweeping circle of the tank, and turns sideways to look at us when she passes the raft. She's quite a bit smaller than the dolphins at the Largo Center. And maybe because she's been sick, her skin isn't as tight and slick as those dolphins'. Her wake creates small waves that wash over the raft, wetting Zoe's shorts and T-shirt and my flip-flops.

Zoe laughs. "Yikes, that's cold."

"Ready?" Don balances Adam on the rim of the tank. When I nod, he puts his hands in Adam's arm-pits and lowers him until I can get my hands around his waist.

Adam flops down beside Zoe and holds his arms out, too. I sit beside him and hold on to his Kid Keeper harness. Just in case.

Both Adam and Zoe are creating a chorus of clicks, squeaks, and whistles no dolphin could resist. Nori tail-stands at the edge of the raft, directly in front of Adam.

"She's on your right," I say to Zoe.

Zoe swings her arm and whacks Adam in the side of the head. He's too focused to notice.

Nori squeezes air through her blowhole, making a sound like a human fart. Adam imitates it; Zoe and I laugh. Nori does it again, only longer and louder, like a foghorn. Adam mimics her.

I remember from the article in the paper that she came from a pod of wild dolphins that visited handicapped children. I wonder if she knows Adam is like the kids who came to see her in the Gulf. I glance up at Don, who's leaning on the side watching. He smiles down at me.

I turn when Zoe giggles. Nori's snout is an inch from her left eye socket, then moves to the right one.

"Isn't that amazing?" Zoe laughs. "She knows they're not real."

Nori sinks away, then swims the pool in a series of tight circles, which rock the raft and create waves that wash up the side of the tank and splash us. The water is icy cold on our hot skin. Adam shrieks with laughter, then mimics the raspberry sound, trying to lure her back.

I tell Zoe everything Nori does and warn her when another wave is coming. When Nori dives, I tell Zoe I can see her circling the bottom and I think she's going to shoot to the surface and do a flip or something, but her blowhole opens and a bubble of air escapes. She touches it with her snout, and it becomes a ring of air. She pushes it toward the surface, but keeps it from reaching the top and bursting. Every time she touches it, it breaks apart, leaving a smaller ring.

"Adam, do you see what she's doing?" To Zoe, I say, "She's blown a bubble of air like a smoke ring and is playing with it."

Adam pulls himself forward on the raft, and I tighten my grip on his harness. He puts his face in the water and blows bubbles. Nori floats toward us. When her blowhole is just beneath the surface, she opens it and a huge bubble of air explodes on the surface.

"We need to get going," Don says.

I look up and he taps his watch.

This will be fun. "You tell Adam."

"Another five minutes, then we have to go."

"What's she doing now?" Zoe asks.

"Blowing bubble rings and bringing them to Adam. He's trying to hook one before it bursts on the surface."

"Poor thing. Isn't there anything in here she can play with?"

"No. There's nothing." I put my hand on Zoe's arm. "When we go back up, be careful what you say. Don wants Adam to be allowed to come see Nori while she's here, so don't say anything more about how awful this tank is, okay?"

"Sure. I'm sorry."

"It's okay." I stand. "Adam, we have to go home."

Of course, he doesn't budge, but I know he heard me, because the level of his squeaks, squeals, and raspberries goes up.

"Lily, I really am sorry. Pinch me or something when you see me talking too much. Please. I don't want your stepfather mad at me. I want us to be friends."

"Me, too, but I *will* pinch you next time."

I take her hand to help her stand and guide her across the raft to the ladder. "You go up first. It's going to be a fight to get Adam away from Nori."

In that second my back was turned, Adam launched himself off the raft.

"Adam!" Don shouts. "Lily, get him."

Adam can swim, but this is a wild dolphin, and she's zooming straight for him.

I step to the edge of the raft, ready to dive in, when Nori comes up under Adam, drapes him across her forehead, and pushes him back to the raft. I lift him out and, before he can stop giggling, I carry him to the ladder and lift him high enough for Don to grab him. As Adam screams and kicks, I turn back to Nori, kneel, and hold my hand out. "Thank you." She nudges my palm.

Don carries a shrieking, sopping-wet Adam toward the back gate. Zoe waits for me, but when I hear Nori whistling, I go back to the rim of the tank. Zoe hears her, too, and comes to stand beside me.

"What's she doing?"

"Trying to get us to stay longer."

Nori dives. I see her blow a bubble ring and push it toward the raft.

"Oh." I grab Zoe's arm.

"What?"

"She made another bubble ring."

"Oh, Lily."

"I know. She's lonely."

On the other side of the wall, a loudspeaker announces

the start of the dolphin show. I hear applause and children's voices.

"I'm so sorry," I say to Nori. "When you get better, you'll go home to your mom."

"I bet they keep her," Zoe says.

"No, they won't." I want to pinch her. "They can't. She has family in the Gulf."

"Don't you think all these dolphins had families?"

I don't want to think about that, and I'm tempted to remind her that this place took Nori in and treated her cancer. She'd be dead right now if it wasn't for them.

PART III

CHAPTER 17

Bayside Oceanarium

Every week, Nori hears a motor like that of the boat that used to bring the little humans to swim with her family. Instead, the sound means the water level in this tank that walls her off from everything she's ever known will drop, sucked out through the frightening hole in the bottom. When it's empty and she's lying on the hard surface with the sun beating down, three or four humans put on masks and climb down into the tank. They wear white boots, like the fishermen on the Gulf used to wear, and they carry the same white buckets, but these are full of bitter liquid instead of the seawater they scooped to wash the fish blood off their decks. These men carry long wooden poles with thick bristles at one end, and hoses. Nori was terrified the first time, and slapped her flukes against the hard concrete, calling frantically for her mother.

One of the humans keeps her skin wet, while the others dip the bristled pole into the buckets and scrub the walls with a liquid, the vapors of which burn Nori's eyes and nostril. Some of it splashes on her, and it stings.

After they have cleaned the walls and washed her bowel movements toward the hole in the bottom of the tank, the man who removed the growth from her jaw joins them. He pries her beak open, looks under her tongue, and washes her mouth out with nasty-tasting liquid. After he leaves, the motor starts again and her prison begins to fill with water to which a yellow, eye-stinging chemical is added.

The only other human she's seen is the one who visits twice daily and throws her dead fish. She's learned that a group of humans means they will empty the water in her tank; a single human will feed her.

But today, Nori is curious about this group of humans, and when one of the young females leaves the others to walk the perimeter of her tank, she follows. The girl clicks to her like another dolphin and speaks softly. She's not here to feed her, but she's not here to empty the pool, either.

When the other girl helps the little boy human see over the top of the tank, Nori's heart races ahead of her mind. Has a boat come? Is it on the other side of this solid circle? Nori now knows how a school of mullet feels when dolphins surround them with a mud-net.

Fish, especially mullet, school together for protection. To capture them in shallow waters, Nori's mother taught her to swim in a circle, beating her tail against the sand. The fish can't see a way through the sand and are easy to catch. When Nori first came here, she used her sonar to look for a way out of this solid sand circle, but it bounced back to her from all directions. Nori gave up calling to her mother many days ago. All she hears is the loud, rhythmic sounds of music during the day, but at night she hears other dolphins somewhere on the other side of the wall. She whistles her mother's name, but there is never an answer.

She has considered dying. If she were brave enough, she could hold her breath and die, but it's hard to let go of the hope that her mother is waiting for her. Then the young humans came and reminded her of home and her family, so she waits.

CHAPTER 18

Miami

No wonder Don called to get me excused from school. Suzanne and I are taking Adam to his first day at the Cutler Academy. Don's not going.

Adam, never easy to feed or dress, is horrible this morning—like he knows something's up even though I try to keep my routine the same: I put his little diapered rear end in his high chair, so I don't have to dress him twice, and give him a ripe banana. The riper the better, as far as he's concerned. He likes to mash it with his fingers, and spread it all over his face. I'm not sure any gets into his stomach, which means he'll be hungry about the time we get to the school. I wonder if it would be child abuse to tube him like they did the prisoners at Guantanamo who went on a hunger strike.

He likes Cheerios, so I pour some on his tray; he wipes them to the floor with a sweep of his banana-slimed hand.

"You're a monster."

He bares his teeth at the two Cheerios he missed. "Grrrrrr."

I thought Don was doing rounds at the hospital, but when the automatic gate opens to let Suzanne in, he comes out of his office.

"I'm going to move his booster seat."

I swear he was hiding in there to let me battle Adam alone. "If you're not going to the hospital, why aren't you coming with us?"

He stops at the back door. "I have a surgery after lunch."

I'm not sure I believe him. Surgeries are usually early in the morning. I give him a yeah-sure look, which he ignores.

When I turn around, Adam flings a chunk of banana at me. It hits me dead center on my forehead, clings for a moment to my face, then slides down my nose and plops onto the top of my left sandal.

I put a hand on either side of his tray, lean right into his face, and snarl, "I hate you."

He turns his head and sinks his teeth into my arm.

I cry out and clamp my hand over the deep white arches. "That does it." I jerk the tray off his chair, snatch him up, and carry him shrieking down the hall to the bathroom. I throw a washcloth into the tub and turn on the water. He screams and kicks, and tries to bite me again, but I hold his arms above his head, his wrists crushed in my fist, and wash his face and chest—not too gently. His shrieks are deafening, and he stomps his feet until they slip out from under him and he lands on his butt in the tub.

I've worn myself out and let go of his arms to wash the banana off my face and out of my hair. While I'm on my knees beside the tub with my face buried in the washcloth, he climbs over the side and runs down the hall, smack into Don, leaving a wet print of himself on Don's pant leg. The print he leaves looks so fragile and small compared to Don's long leg.

"How come he's not ready? You're going to be late."

I reach over and slam the bathroom door.

* * * * * *

Nothing I try seems to distract Adam from trying to escape. I put his *Little Dolphin* book and the cleanest of his stuffed dolphins in his diaper bag. When he sees them, he grabs and throws them across the room, knocking over a lamp with the book.

I resort to putting him in his Kid Keeper harness and leash, but when Suzanne sees it, she shakes her head. "I hate to see children in those things."

"If you think you can control him, have at it," I say. "He bit me this morning."

"Did you bite him back?" Her eyes twinkle.

I try to smile. "I wanted to." I look at my feet, then at her, and suck on my bottom lip. "I told him I hated him. I don't really. Do you think he understood me?"

"No, I don't." Suzanne puts her arm around my shoulders. "It's going to get better, toots. Trust me. Sending Adam to school is a huge step for Dr. Don. Once he sees the difference it makes, he'll be onboard."

"You think it will make a difference?"

"Your brother is going to be autistic all of his life. There are no miracle cures, and nothing will change that, but his life, yours, and Don's will be better for the training he gets there."

Suzanne always leaves me feeling hopeful.

The Cutler Academy is in Pinecrest, south of South Miami. We were supposed to be there at nine; by the time we pull in, it's already ten.

With Adam under my arm, his leash dragging behind us, I run toward the building while Suzanne searches for a parking place. The door is locked. I wrap Adam's leash tightly around my hand, put him down, and knock. Elisa, the director, opens the door.

"I'd about given up on you."

"We had a tough morning. I'm sorry."

"Not a problem. We're having our morning snack break, and there's a place at the table for Adam." Elisa turns to watch Suzanne coming up the walkway. "What's that?" She points at the diaper bag.

"I brought his favorite book, one of his stuffed dolphins, and his diapers," I explain.

"I suppose this is my fault, but I'm pretty sure I told your father—"

"He's my stepfather."

"I told your stepfather, we can't take children who aren't toilet trained."

"What?"

Suzanne trots up, looks at the expression on my face, then at Elisa. "What?"

"He's not toilet trained. I'm sorry. I can't ask our teachers to change diapers."

There's a railing attached to the handicapped ramp. I sag against it and turn pleadingly to Suzanne.

"I'm his nanny. If I stay, can he?"

Elisa looks at Adam, who is trying to pry my fingers

off the grip I have on his leash. He's dancing with frustration and begins to cry.

My heart pounds. I don't think I can stand it if she says no.

She must see the desperation I feel on my face. She pats my arm where the print of Adam's teeth is now two bruised arcs; to Suzanne she says, "If you can come with him every day, I'll make an exception."

I close my eyes.

CHAPTER 19

Three children sit in a semicircle around the table where the boys were making flowers on that first visit. Daniel, Roberto, and the little girl whose name I don't know each have a plate and a carton of apple juice in front of them. The teachers glance at us when we come in, but not the children. I can't remember the last time Adam saw another kid his age or size.

Suzanne has his hand, so I unsnap the leash from his harness. He jerks free, runs to the nearest table, and crawls under it. He presses his back to the wall, draws his legs up, and clamps his hands into his armpits.

"Leave him there," Elisa says. "I'd rather see him come out on his own."

"I want," a mechanical voice says.

Tall, skinny Roberto, the oldest of the children by about four years, sits last at the table. A teacher sits next to him.

In front of him is a green box called a GoTalk Communicator 4. It's a battery-operated recorder and picture box. The top square on the left says I WANT. Below are four pictures, three of food choices—apple, goldfish, cereal—the fourth is the word *tickle*. The top square on the right says ALL DONE.

Roberto pushes the cereal-box picture and the voice says, "Cereal."

The teacher pours out a little pile of Cheerios. Roberto puts a few in his mouth, then pushes the I WANT button again, then TICKLE.

"Chew and swallow first," the teacher says.

He does, then pushes I WANT and TICKLE again.

"Show me your mouth."

He opens wide and twists in his seat to give her the best view.

"Good boy." She reaches over and dances her fingers up and down his ribs. He doubles over, giggling.

A teacher turns her attention to Daniel. "Daniel, can you touch your nose?"

He stops rocking and touches his nose with his index finger.

Elisa, who's standing beside me, says, "Asking them to do something helps them focus."

"Excellent, Daniel. Now can you show me what you want to eat?"

I glance at Adam. He's still in the same place but is moving his head from side to side and tapping his lips with clumped fingers—the sign for *eat*.

Elisa sees it, too. "How many sign words does he know?"

"Two: *eat* and *drink*."

"That's a start."

"My stepfather thinks it will delay him learning to talk."

"Any form of communication lessens frustration and probably speeds up the process of learning to speak."

Elisa squats down. "Adam, there's a chair for you at the table. Are you hungry?" She signs *eat*.

Adam puts his fingers in his ears and rolls his head from side to side.

"Well, come out if you want something to eat." Elisa stands up and turns her back to him.

I follow her lead and turn my back, too.

I hear Adam's feet clump, clump on the floor as he scoots out from under the table. I glance back at him. He's at the edge, between two of the legs. I sign *eat*, but he ignores me. He's watching the little girl at the table, then catches sight of his diaper bag, which is on the floor next to Suzanne's leg. The dolphin's head is sticking out. Adam flaps his hands and squeaks.

"He wants his dolphin," Suzanne says.

Elisa takes it out of the bag and puts it in the empty chair at the table.

Adam starts to scream and bang his heels on the floor.

Elisa takes the dolphin, gets a clear plastic container down from a high shelf in one of the rooms, and puts it inside.

Adam's eyes follow her while she puts the container back on the shelf. I think he's going to lose it, but he looks at his hand flapping against his own palm and squeaks. Before I have a chance to realize something different just happened, he crawls out from under the table, walks over, and looks up at his dolphin in the plastic bin. He points, then starts his pre-meltdown jig.

Elisa walks over, squats in front of him, and brings clumped fingers to her lips. "We eat first, Adam, then you can play with your dolphin."

Adam screams like he's been burned with a lit match, leans over, and head-butts her. Caught off balance, she falls over. He kicks her in the shoulder before either Suzanne or I can react. I grab for him, but he twists away and dives under another table, curls into a ball, and shrieks.

Once again my heart is pounding so hard I can see my pulse through the skin of my wrist. Not only is he not potty trained, but he's turning violent and dangerous. "I'm so sorry." I hold a hand out to help her up.

"Don't think a thing about it. It's actually pretty typical."

I blurt, "Thank heavens."

She smiles and takes my hand.

CHAPTER 20

When Suzanne, who's carrying a sleeping Adam, and I come in from the Cutler Academy, Don turns from staring out the window over the sink. He hasn't shaved, his hair is a mess, and his eyes are red.

"What's wrong?"

My emotional bank-vault of a stepfather shakes his head. "Nothing. How'd it go?"

It was a nightmare, but I glance at Suzanne and say, "Pretty good."

Suzanne nods, turns, and carries Adam down the hall to his room.

"Really? Why's he asleep?" He looks at his watch. "It's only one."

"He had a bit of a meltdown." This isn't a huge lie. It only lasted forty-five minutes, but what it lacked in duration, it made up for in an all-time effort and volume. He screamed until he hyperventilated and couldn't breathe. Suzanne pinned his arms while Elisa cupped her hand over his nose and mouth and held his head still until his breathing got back to normal. I stood there thinking about how happy he is with any dolphin. I want to believe, like that woman at the Largo Center said, that he needs both, but in contrast to swimming with the dolphins, this is a nightmare.

Then I remembered Mom once said that life is full of hills we have to climb. I was young enough to think she meant autism was one of those hills and that once Adam reached the top, he'd start back toward being a normal little boy again on his way down the other side. Only in my dreams. Of course, in those, Mom is still alive. I sometimes think I'm as deep in denial about how his mind works and what it will take to reach him as Don is.

Suzanne comes back down the hall. "Did you tell him about that thing Roberto was using?"

I shake my head.

Don looks from me to Suzanne and back.

"It was a battery-operated box with pictures of food," I say.

Suzanne goes to the sink, squirts liquid soap onto a sponge, and turns on the water. "Roberto is eight—"

"Oh, Jesus," Don says. "And he still can't talk?"

"It's different. He's autistic and has cerebral palsy. He uses it to tell the therapists what he wants to eat."

"What's it called?" Don looks worse than the day Momma died.

"GoTalk something or other," I say.

"GoTalk Communicator 4," Suzanne says. "I wrote it down." She wipes one hand on a dish towel, digs in her sweatpants' pocket, and gives Don a scrap of paper with a grocery list on the other side. "I bet you could get one online."

Don folds and puts it in his pocket. "Thanks."

"Are you going to order one?" I ask.

Don shrugs. "It's like sign language. If you make it easy for him to communicate in other ways, he'll never talk. I want to hear him speak." He presses his lips together for a moment. "Maybe hear him call me Daddy."

Dada was the first word Adam learned and, as well as I can remember, the last I heard him speak.

Suds and steam rise from the sink. Suzanne turns off the water. "That's what I thought, too, but the therapist said any form of communication lessens frustration and might speed up the process of learning to talk."

Don sighs.

"Is something wrong?" Suzanne asks. "You look awful."

"I . . . I lost a patient this morning."

I glance at the clock on the oven; it's a little after one. He was supposed to have a surgery at noon. "The one you were going to operate on?"

He nods.

"I'm sorry," Suzanne and I say at the same time.

"What happened?"

He shakes his head. Don doesn't talk about the patients he loses, or those he saves. The only way I know he's lost one is when he goes out dressed in his only dark suit, the one he puts on for funerals.

From down the hall, Adam begins to cry.

Suzanne dries her hands and goes to get him.

I don't know how I know the patient who died was a child and a boy, but I do. "How old was he?"

"Five."

I go stand beside Don. He doesn't move, clear his throat, or anything, so I put my arm around his waist and lean my head against his shoulder.

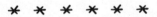

Suzanne made a big salad before she left for home. Don cooked two steaks on the grill. At dinner he says, "I went by to check on Nori today. She's doing great. They are going to move her from that tank into a pond. It's much nicer."

"So she's cured?"

"You never know with cancer."

"When will they release her back to her family?"

"I want to leave all our options open, Lily." He's picking the green peppers out of his salad.

"What does that mean? You're not pulling Adam out of Cutler, are you?"

"No. He can do both."

"Both?"

"The Oceanarium used to have a dolphin-assisted therapy program, and they think Nori's a good candidate for trying it again. The therapist is still in the area, and she's interested in coming back to work."

Adam's crazy happy around dolphins—as happy as he ever gets, so maybe a program like that could help him. But what Zoe said about Nori having a family nags me. "Don't they have to release her if she's cured?"

"She's not *cured*, Lily. Her cancer is in remission." Don's got all the peppers in a little pile on the side of his plate. "Want these?"

"No. I don't like them, either."

"Why don't you tell Suzanne to stop putting them in?"

"Why don't you?"

"I forget."

"So do I."

Don grins. "Shall I have my secretary send her a memo?"

I don't think of Don as having a sense of humor, but since he smiled, I'm going to assume he's kidding. "That's probably the only way it will get done."

"How about we go visit Nori again on Saturday? If she's doing all right in her new home, Adam can swim with her. Zoe can come if you like. And Suzanne, if she wants."

I shrug. I've finally got the two things I wanted—a new friend and help for Adam. Too bad they're not compatible. "Zoe warned me this would happen, so I'm not sure inviting her is a good idea."

Don gets that smirky look on his face that I hate. "What did Zoe warn you would happen?"

"That the Oceanarium would keep Nori."

"Maybe she'll feel differently when she sees how nice Nori's new home is. But don't invite her if you don't want to."

"No, I want to. How does dolphin-assisted therapy work, anyway?"

"I don't know, and frankly, I don't care. Seeing Adam happy is all that matters. Whatever benefit can be gained is—" He looks at the overcooked chunk of steak on his fork. "Gravy. Which this meat could also use."

It occurs to me that this will be all about Adam, and I may not even get to swim with Nori. Don must mistake the expression on my face for concern about Zoe.

"Ask Zoe this: Which is more important, your brother or that dolphin?"

The answer is Adam, of course, but I don't think this is an either-or thing. I wish I knew more about it so I can get it settled in my mind.

*　*　*　*　*　*

The last thing I do before turning out my light at night is check on Adam. I email Zoe to invite her to come with us on Saturday, then tiptoe down the hall to his room. His door's open, and Don's standing at the foot of his bed.

I go in. "Whatcha doing?"

"Watching him sleep."

"I do that, too, sometimes."

"He looks so normal."

"I know."

Don's grief for the little boy he lost today and for Adam is etched on his face.

"I'm sorry about your patient."

"He was such a little trouper."

"What kind of cancer did he have?"

"Brain stem glioma. I removed the first tumor when he was three."

"And it came back?"

"In his brain."

"How do you know when they're cured for good?"

"Never."

"You mean Zoe's cancer could come back?"

Don looks at me, and his expression changes to that mask he wears. "Highly unlikely."

"But it could."

"Lily, cancer can never be cured, but full remission can last a lifetime."

"And Nori?"

"Same thing. Honestly, that's the best reason to keep her. She'll have better medical care than most humans, and if there's a recurrence, she'll be treated. In the wild, if it comes back, she'll die."

Adam suddenly giggles, but he's still asleep.

I smile at Don. "Do you think his subconscious heard us say her name?"

"Could be."

"I feel sorry for Nori."

"You shouldn't. She'll have a long, safe life."

"So you think it's better to live no matter what, even

if the way you have to live is not so great, than to live well and die when you're supposed to?"

"You're asking the wrong person. I've always got a dog in the fight."

"What does that mean?"

"It's a metaphor. It means I have a vested interest in my son, my patients, and now in Nori."

CHAPTER 21

I come home from school on Tuesday to find Adam naked in the backyard, playing with his stuffed dolphins. There's an empty tuna can leaning against the base of our palm tree, which shades the lawn chair where Suzanne sits watching him. Mrs. Walden's at her kitchen window, holding her cat like she's sharing an entertaining event. The hedge has some new growth, so I imagine she's on her tiptoes trying not to miss a thing.

"Why's he naked?"

Suzanne grins. "Stage one of housebreaking Adam."

"With a tuna can?"

"It's the target."

I sit down next to her. "How's this supposed to work?"

"Well, I'm not sure. I mean, I know how to get started, but I need Dr. Don's help."

"Did you ask him?"

"Not yet. I was waiting for you to come home."

"What can I do?"

Suzanne glances at Mrs. Walden at her kitchen window. "Go ask him to come pee in that can."

I laugh. "You're kidding?"

Her expression is totally serious. "I am not. It's how my husband—God rest his soul—toilet trained our son."

I grin, glance again in the direction of our neighbor, and run into the house. Don's in his office. "Suzanne needs you."

"What for?"

I shrug, and leave before he can see my big, fat grin.

I hear him sigh, push his chair back, and follow me across the living room.

The first thing Don does when he sees Adam's naked little butt and the tuna can is glance at Mrs. Walden's kitchen window. She's put the cat down and must have pulled a stool over because she's leaning over her sink with her nose practically pressed to the glass.

"What going on here?"

"Suzanne thinks she can house . . . toilet train Adam."

Suzanne seems a little less confident now that Don's standing with his hands on his hips. "It's how my husband potty trained our son."

"What's the can for?"

"Something to aim at," Suzanne says.

"Okay." It hasn't dawned on him what she wants.

Suzanne looks at me. She saved us from getting tossed out of the Cutler Academy, so I owe her one. "He needs an example, someone to show him what to do."

Don looks at me over the top of his reading glasses. "Is this a joke?"

"You need to pee in that can," I say.

Don stares at the can, glances over at Mrs. Walden, then smiles. "A little privacy, please." He waves us off.

Suzanne gets up, and together we walk toward the house.

"Adam, watch Daddy."

The next thing I hear is pee hitting the can like a downpour on a tin roof, then a lopped-off cry from Mrs. Walden's house, followed by the clatter of a dish breaking.

"Can you do that?" Don says to Adam.

I have to peek.

With his hands on Adam's shoulders, Don has pulled him over to face the tuna can. "Go ahead. Give it a try."

Adam pees on his own bare feet and the toes of Don's flip-flops, then starts to hop up and down and giggle.

Suzanne said yes to joining us on Saturday at the Oceanarium, and will take Adam to see the manatees until Don and the vet finish their meeting. That means Zoe and I are free to go watch the dolphin show.

Don drops us at the front entrance, where we're to wait for an escort to take us in. While we're waiting, two school buses pull up and unload about a hundred screaming kids. Adam claps his hands over his ears and screws up his face. Before he has a chance to lose it, Suzanne picks him up and carries him away.

One of the girls from the bus notices Zoe's cane and grabs a friend's arm to point her out. I glare at her even though I know Zoe doesn't care that people stare. I did exactly the same thing the first time I saw her.

I wonder if we'd get bored with staring at obvious differences if all our physical and emotional losses were in plain sight. I could get *motherless* tattooed on my forehead, or start a line of T-shirts.

A sullen-looking Oceanarium employee comes out of the exit gate, looks at the crowd of teenagers, and rolls his eyes. The shirt I'd make for him would say, *I hate this job.*

I take Zoe's arm and signal Suzanne, then we follow him to the front of the line past all those kids. "They're comps," he says to the ticket-taker.

She inspects us with a disapproving glare.

Once inside, he walks away without a word, but stops about ten yards ahead and turns to stare at Zoe.

"I love how boys can't take their eyes off me."

I laugh. "How'd you know?" Boys see right through me, so I wonder if Zoe really does like them looking at her or is creeped out because she can't see them. When I know her better, I'll ask.

She grins. "He's wearing eau de fish and his sneakers squeak."

He realizes we're talking about him, blushes, and walks away. His shoes do squeak. I hadn't noticed.

Adam makes a beeline for a kiosk selling hideous pink-and-blue inflatable dolphins. He stares up at them twisting in the breeze, flaps his hands, and makes raspberries. Suzanne picks him up and carries him toward the entrance. She puts him down when he starts to buck, and jogs after him, holding tight to his Kid Keeper leash.

When we catch up, Adam is hugging the tail of a bronze dolphin, one of a pair, both of which are about nine feet tall. I get Zoe to stand beside him, and I take a picture with my cell phone.

Everything looks the same as when Mom and I were here three years ago. We enter through a pair of giant shark jaws. Straight ahead is a bank of windows with an underwater view of dolphins in a tank. One of them seems to be scratching its face on a huge pipe. Another glides by the window.

I don't get a chance to describe any of this to Zoe before a blaring announcement for the upper-deck dolphin show crackles over the speakers. I guide Zoe toward the stairs.

This show must not draw big crowds; there are no bleachers and no place to sit. People can stand at the railing around the tank, and risk getting wet, or on one of the two levels of metal steps that form a semicircle above the walkway. It's only ten thirty, but the sun is already broiling hot. We walk to the side with an overhang and a little shade.

Kiss's "Rock and Roll All Nite" screams over the staticky speakers while three girls in turquoise-and-black wet suits stand in the front half of a pirate ship, tossing tiny bits of fish to the dolphins. I count six dolphins gathered below the ship's bow, all chattering with their mouths open. Gulls circle overhead in anticipation of the feeding. One swoops in and snatches a piece of fish before the dolphin can catch it.

Zoe's holding on to the railing with both hands. She looks pale and her knuckles are white.

"Are you okay?"

She nods. "It's the noise. I'll be okay."

Duh. She relies on hearing to orient herself, so of course the loud music, kids laughing and shouting to each other, and the noise of people filling the metal stands makes her dizzy. No wonder Zoe understands Adam better than we do.

"How big is the tank?" she shouts next to my ear.

"I don't know. Not very."

"How big?"

I know I'm her eyes, but I want to have fun today. "Twice the size of our pool, Zoe. Okay?" Then I feel bad for sounding cross, so I tell her where the six dolphins are, and how the girls are tossing them fish.

"They line up like that because they're hungry," she says.

"How do you know?"

"I've been reading about it online. That's how they train dolphins and get them to do tricks. They keep them hungry."

Before I can tell Zoe to chill, one of the girls puts on a microphone and shouts out a welcome. "Our dolphins are big show-offs," she shouts. The three girls signal the dolphins and they all lift out of the water, tail-walk backward across the pool, dive, and race to the pirate ship for their reward. After that, one at a time, the dolphins take turns doing flips, tail-walking, and splashing the people who chose to stand at the railing. All this brings shrieks and laughter from the crowd.

Two of the girls in the pirate ship keep the dolphins that are not performing occupied by tossing them small pieces of fish. The one that does the trick gets a whole fish when it returns. Zoe turns her back on the show and stands facing into the breeze. There's a thunderhead out over the water to our east, and she's sniffing the air.

"Our dolphins are trivia buffs," announces the trainer. "This is my team." She pans the dolphins with her hand. "Let's see if you"—she means the audience—"can answer before they do." She holds up a finger. "Question number one: Dolphins are fish." The dolphins shake their heads from side to side a moment before the audience shouts, "False."

"That's right—but my team got it first. Question number two." She holds up two fingers, a signal to the dolphins, I'm sure. "The hole on top of a dolphin's head is called a blowhole." The dolphins nod; the audience yells, "True."

"The show's kind of dumb," I say.

Zoe nods. "I've got ears."

"All our girl dolphins are moms," shouts the girl with the microphone. "We like to think of Troy, our only male, as one very lucky boy to have five beautiful girlfriends. Take a bow, Troy." The trainer lifts her arm and Troy dives, then sails into the air.

Zoe turns and says loud enough for people around us to hear. "Are you kidding me?"

"Shhhh, Zoe. People are looking."

"I don't care. Does it occur to anyone to ask where their babies are?"

The guy one level down from us has his kid balanced on the railing in front of him. He turns to look at Zoe. I think he's going to tell her to put a cork in it, but he nods in agreement and says, "I was thinking the same thing, young lady."

✳ ✳ ✳ ✳ ✳ ✳

We're following the last of the audience down the steps from the upper deck. When we reach the bottom, Zoe turns. "I'm sorry about up there. I should keep my big mouth shut. I'm ruining this for you. Please don't be mad."

"I'm not mad."

"Are you sure?"

"Pretty sure."

"Then you are mad." Zoe lets her hand drop from my shoulder.

Zoe's as passionate about the dolphins as I am about

doing what's best for my brother. "It's just . . . I have to be on my brother's side. If Cutler Academy doesn't help Adam, then maybe Nori will. At least here she'll be safe and well cared for."

Zoe finds my arm and takes my hand. "Don't be mad, okay. I won't say another word, I promise." She zips her lips.

"Did I tell you that I was here with my mother a year before she died?" I don't mention that Mom didn't like it, either.

"Oh, Lily, I'm sorry. I really should shut up."

CHAPTER 22

I'm worried about how Suzanne is managing with Adam. There's so much going on: show announcements, employees hawking photo ops with the animals, music pulsing from different directions like an orchestra tuning up endlessly and loudly, kids running and screaming, birds screeching, and the hot, humid air thick with greasy food smells. I can't imagine Adam is coping well.

Suzanne said they'd be at the manatee tank, but no one's there except a girl tossing heads of romaine lettuce into the water. The three manatees munch on the fresh lettuce heads that bob among the remains of a prior feeding.

We leave and wander through the Oceanarium until I see Suzanne waving from the stingray exhibit. Adam is mesmerized and doesn't look up when we join them.

"Has Don called you?"

Suzanne shakes her head.

"I wonder what's taking him so long."

The stingray tank is long and shallow, with a pile of fern-covered rocks at one end. A ship's anchor and more rocks decorate a center island. The water is a weak tea color, but still clear enough to see the sand and gravel on the bottom. The whole exhibit is completely covered with a canvas canopy. It's as close to cool and breezy under it as it ever gets in Miami in June.

Adam's shirt is soaking wet. "Did he fall in?"

Suzanne smiles. "Just wait."

I stare at the water. Stingrays sweep by counterclockwise in groups of threes and fours. Adam starts to giggle, arches his back, and pokes his belly out. One of the rays upends, exposing a creamy white belly, and looks like it is going to sprout limbs and crawl over the edge. Its eyes and mouth look like a smiley-face emoticon. It suddenly flaps its wings and splashes water in a wave over the side, soaking Adam's T-shirt, pants, and shoes.

I burst out laughing.

"What?" Zoe says.

I pull her over and stand her beside Adam. "You'll see."

It takes a minute for the stingray to make a complete loop around the tank. They all look alike to me, but

Adam sees his stingray coming and starts to giggle. I make sure Zoe is close enough to the tank so when it flaps its wings this time, it will get them both. Adam and Zoe shriek with laughter.

"What did that?" Zoe's still laughing.

"One of the stingrays."

I look at Suzanne, and see in her eyes exactly what I'm thinking. This is all I want for my brother—to be a happy, laughing little boy. She pats my arm and smiles. "You okay?" She tucks a loose strand of hair behind my ear.

"Yeah." But tears threaten. My mother was always doing that—tucking my hair behind an ear, and as soon as she turned her back, I'd shake it free again.

* * * * * *

Thunder has been rumbling, and now it starts to sprinkle. Don still hasn't called, and when I try his number, it goes to voice mail, so we walk the short distance to the golden-domed sea lion show.

Two-thirds of the gold geodesic dome is an open weave, like a metal spiderweb. The other third is covered with sheeting painted gold. We climb all the way to the top to find seats out of the rain. From there I can see the four pools, including the one Nori is in. Was in. It's empty.

Rain begins to hammer the metal sheeting of the dome, and the people sitting in the open get up and climb toward us, including the kids from the buses, all screaming and running like their skin is being burned off. We end up packed like germs in a head cold under the covered third of the dome.

Suzanne has an umbrella. She opens it and holds it angled against the wind that's kicked up. Down below, the show goes on. Salty plays catch with a beach ball, balancing it on his nose and tossing it back with a jerk of his head.

My phone rings. It's Don.

"I'm with Nori," he says.

"Where's that?"

"On the far east side. Do you know where Adam and Suzanne are?"

Lightning flashes, causing the phone to crackle. Then thunder booms.

"They're here with us."

"How's he doing?"

I glance at Adam. The trainer's voice, amplified by the microphone, is high-pitched. Music blares, the sea lion is too far away to hold Adam's attention, too many people are too close, and thunder is booming. He's got his hands over his ears and has started to twist from side to side.

"He's fine."

"When the rain stops, bring him over here so they can get him suited up to swim." The phone goes dead.

"Don's with Nori." I show Suzanne where that is on the map. "We'll follow when the rain stops."

"Adam, let's go see your dolphin." She picks him up, shields him with the umbrella, and starts down the wet steps.

We came in on the left side of the dome, but Suzanne sees there's a closer exit on the right and takes it. If she hadn't, I might not have noticed the series of small tanks behind a tall board fence. We're so high up in the stands that I can see over it. A large bull sea lion—another Salty, no doubt—is in a tiny, probably eight-by-ten, concrete tank. There's chain-link fencing on three sides and the board fence on the side meant to hide him from the audience. Again and again, he leaps out of the water in an attempt to scale the wall of his tank. His situation is such a contrast to the setting they've created at the entrance for public consumption that I glance at Zoe, forgetting that she can't see. I watch the sea lion jump and fall back, jump and fall back, while the Salty on stage climbs a set of stairs behind phony rocks and comes down a slide into the water.

✳ ✳ ✳ ✳ ✳ ✳

The sun is out, and steam rises off every stone surface as Zoe and I walk to where the Oceanarium keeps the dolphins people can swim with.

"Welcome," says a guy behind the ticket counter. "Are you here for Dolphin Encounter or Dolphin Odyssey?" He sees Zoe's cane, leans and whispers to the person next to him. "Can she do a swim-with?"

"I'm blind, not deaf."

"I meant there are . . . um . . . physical restrictions."

I hear Adam screaming in a changing room.

Maybe it's because of that sea lion, but I see this building, all clean and modern with a fancy gift shop, a separate ticket counter, and people who smile at us when we come in, as just another board fence, here to block our view to what this place is really about.

"I'm not sure," I say. "What's the difference between the encounter and the odyssey?"

Zoe smiles. She knows we're not paying for anything.

"The Dolphin Encounter is an hour-and-a-half shallow-water experience for a hundred and thirty-five dollars. Plus tax," he adds. "You get to train and feed the dolphins, kiss them, and shake hands. The Dolphin Odyssey is an hour-and-a-half deep-water experience for a hundred and ninety-nine dollars, plus tax. It includes everything in the encounter and you can swim with them." He looks at Zoe. "Observers are only fifty-four dollars."

The door to the restroom swings open, and a frazzled-looking Suzanne appears with Adam, who is crammed into a wet suit. Everyone turns to look at a kicking, shrieking black-and-blue sausage.

"Are you together?" the guy behind the counter asks.

I nod.

He gives me a dirty look. "Our vet and your father are waiting for you. Out there." He sends us through a set of glass doors in the wall of plate-glass windows.

At first glance, this looks like the nicest place of all for the dolphins. The lagoon is about the size of two Olympic-sized pools side by side. It's landscaped with a dense wall of palms, coral rocks, and white fencing. There's a white-sand bottom as deep as I can see. Out in the center, held up by four white pillars, is a twenty-by-twenty canvas canopy. It creates a small square of shade from the sun.

A closer look and I see that the back half of the pool is divided by water-level chain-link fences into six small pens—with a dolphin in each pen.

Don waves to us from the far side of the enclosure. He's with the vet and a woman who must be the therapist they've hired back to run their dolphin-assisted therapy program. She's about Don's age, but tall and thin enough to look good in the bathing suit she's wearing.

I guide Zoe around the perimeter of the pool, glancing out over the water each time I hear a blow.

A cloud shadow passes, turning the water dark, then bright again.

Don grins and opens his arms. "Nori's new home."

CHAPTER 23

Zoe whispers, "Just tell me, Lily, is it nice?"

"It's not bad."

"How bad is not bad?" Zoe says.

"I thought you were going to let this go."

Zoe drops her hand from my shoulder. "I should probably wait inside." She turns and begins tapping the walkway.

"Zoe. Wait." I get in front of her. Her cheeks glisten. "You're crying."

"I still have tear ducts," she snaps. She wipes her cheeks with the heel of her hand.

"I'm sorry. I just don't know what you want me to do."

"I might have been asking you to describe it to me because I'm blind, not because I was going to slam this place again."

"Yeah, right. That's why you asked 'how bad is not bad.'"

Zoe smiles and I hug her.

"So how bad is it?"

"Don's watching. I'll tell you later."

Adam's straining against the hold Suzanne has on the straps of his life jacket.

"This is . . ." Don turns to the woman. "Is it Dr. Bowman?"

"No." She holds her hand out to Suzanne. "It's Sandi Bowman. Are you the mother?"

"My wife is dead," Don says. "This is Adam's nanny, Suzanne"—he puts a hand on my shoulder—"his sister, Lily, and Lily's friend, Zoe."

I move out from under his hand. Suzanne is more than Adam's nanny and I'm more than the center of our universe's sister.

"How lovely to meet you all." Sandi beams at us with teeth a horse would envy. "I'm so happy to be back at the Oceanarium doing the work I love. Kids and dolphins. What more could one ask for?"

I look at Don like *you've got to be kidding me, this airhead is going to make the difference*, but he's smiling down at Adam, who's lying on his stomach on the dock, arms held out to Nori.

Nori's got a raw-looking cut on top of her beak. "What happened there?" I point to it.

"She probably rammed the fencing," Sandi says. "I don't think it's easy for them to see."

Though it's been two weeks since we were here, Nori obviously recognizes Adam. She blows an air bubble and pushes it toward him.

He pops it, then squeaks and giggles.

"Clearly, they are already friends," Sandi says to Don. "Which is wonderful, since Nori's had no training."

"Is it okay to ask? What does that training involve?" Zoe's tone is as light and airy as Sandi's.

Don gives me a look, which I ignore. "I'd like to know, too." I mimic Zoe's tone.

"Well, it's all based on a system of rewards. Behaviors we want to encourage are rewarded, and undesirable behaviors or failures to perform go unrewarded. It's quite simple."

Zoe was right, they keep the dolphins hungry. But training at the Cutler Academy is based on a similar system. They don't withhold food, but I remember Elisa telling us that they reinforce the behaviors they want the kids to repeat by giving them something they want. Roberto chewed and swallowed his food for a tickle. Adam wants anything dolphin. Which will benefit him more? School or Nori? Or will it take both?

Zoe gets braver. "Does that mean poor Nori goes hungry until she gets it right?"

"Not really. They perform best when they're hungry, but . . ." Sandi smiles at Nori. "Dolphins are so smart, they catch on very quickly."

Nori opens her beak and lets out a stream of clicks and whistles.

Sandi laughs. "See."

Adam is trying to get into the water, straining against the hold Don has on his life jacket.

"Let's get started, shall we?" Sandi sits on the side of the raft, scrunchies her long hair into a ponytail, and slips into the water, which comes only to her waist.

They say animals are great judges of people. Nori dives beneath the surface. When she comes up again, she's against the fence on the far side of the pool—as far away from therapist Sandi as she can get.

"Adam, sit here." She pats the dock.

He twists from side to side.

"Adam, you have to sit here." She puts her hands in his armpits, lifts, and plops him on the dock.

Adam starts to wail and kick, soaking her.

"Lily . . . it is Lily, isn't it? Will you bring that bucket of fish over and put it next to your brother?

"Now, Adam, look at me." With her free hand, Sandi turns his head to face her, but his eyes roll in Nori's direction.

"Adam. Look at me."

He doesn't.

"Nori would like to play with you, but you need to call her over. Can you say 'Nori'?"

As much as I want my brother to talk, I pray with all my might that he doesn't. Not today. That would be all Don needs to seal Nori's fate—if it's not already sealed. I hold my breath.

Adam does a raspberry and flaps his hand.

"Nor-ee," Sandi says.

Adam starts to rock.

"Nor-ee."

He kicks his feet, splashing Sandi.

She wipes her face and catches his ankles.

"Nor-ee."

Adam twists, breaking her grip on his legs, but falls backward, hitting his head on the dock. He shrieks.

Zoe smiles.

Suzanne shakes her head. "Have you had much opportunity to work with autistic children?"

Sandi pulls Adam upright and checks the back of his head. "It either wasn't as prevalent when I was here in the nineties—" She has to shout to be heard over Adam's screams. "Or, if it was, it wasn't diagnosed as often. Many behavioral issues have a great deal in common."

Suzanne's eyes flash when she looks at me.

"Nori's hungry, Adam." Sandi pulls the bucket closer. "Would you like to feed her?"

Adam is beyond hearing her.

Don looks helplessly at Suzanne, who marches over, scoops him up, and carries him to a nearby bench. She sits and places Adam between her knees. I've seen her do this before. She applies pressure, gently but firmly squeezing him with her thighs. Since she came to work for us, she's been reading books about autism, especially ones written by Temple Grandin, who has Asperger's syndrome, a high-functioning form of autism. Temple built herself a squeeze-box when she was in college and would crawl into it when she felt a meltdown coming. It had solid sides, and she could close them down on herself. When Suzanne explained this to me, I told her how Mom used to let Adam sleep in the chest of drawers.

It takes a few minutes, but Adam stops the rhythmic sirenlike shrieking, though he continues to cry. Suzanne whispers next to his ear, "Nori's watching."

Adam sniffles and turns to look at Nori's pool. Sandi has gotten out of the water, and Nori has moved nearer the raft. She's upended and *is* watching Adam. Suzanne lets him go and he runs to the raft.

Sandi claps her hands together. "Are we ready to try again?"

Don catches her arm. "Let's see what happens without making it an exercise."

"Well. Sure. Can't expect miracles the first time out." She laughs.

Adam sits and scoots to the edge of the raft. Nori slides her head up next to him. He stokes her cheek, then gets curious about the hole in the top of her head. When he gets on his knees to look inside, she closes it, then opens it again, luring him closer.

Adam puts a hand on either side of her blowhole, leans over, and cocks his head like he's going to put his eye to the hole. Don reaches to stop him at the same moment Nori blasts him in the face with a puff of air. He falls back, giggles, and begins to pet her again, murmuring incoherently.

I've been giving Zoe a blow-by-blow. When I tell her what Nori did, it dawns on me—Adam got the joke she played on him.

Zoe realizes it, too. Her lips compress, then she turns and walks away.

From the other side of a high board fence, I hear a girl's voice shouting, "Have your picture taken petting a dolphin. Only fifty dollars."

CHAPTER 24

The rest of Saturday and all day Sunday after our visit with Nori, Adam *is* calmer. He plays with his toy dolphins, watches his DVD, and sleeps through the night. By Monday, when Suzanne comes to take him to school, he's as fussy as usual.

Zoe's JAWS program has read the entire 1972 Marine Mammal Act to her, and she basically spent the weekend reciting the whole thing to me. She keeps calling and emailing to tell me more facts. Since it was passed, aquariums haven't been allowed to capture dolphins in American waters, though there's a loophole if they are trapped for vaguely defined "research." None, for any reason, has been taken since 1989. Instead they breed them, which explains what happened to all those baby dolphins at the Oceanarium. They sold them, or put them in the pens for the swim-with-dolphins program.

Yesterday morning's email: *She's a wild dolphin. How come they can keep her?*

Then in the afternoon: *Did you know dolphins can live for 40 years? Can you imagine Nori in that place for another 37 years?*

I can't, but I don't answer.

Today she's burying me with her research on DAT— Dolphin Assisted Therapy.

Zoe: *There's no proof it does anything!! It's nothing but an expensive swim-with program.* There's a link attached.

My answer: *Can we stop talking about this?*

Of course, I'm pretty sure I do know how they're keeping her. The Oceanarium and Don are in cahoots. I don't tell Zoe because I think freeing Nori might be more important to her than our friendship and that she'd risk never being allowed in this house again if it meant saving her.

I keep trying to tell myself that Nori's only one dolphin. There are aquariums all over the world, and thousands of dolphins die in fishing nets every year. Heck, the Japanese eat them. If the AquaPlanet people hadn't found her, Nori would be dead now. For Adam's sake, I think we have to give it a chance to work.

I tell myself that, but I keep thinking about those mother dolphins in that sterile upper-deck tank, scratching an itch on a metal pipe and having their babies taken away from them. And that sea lion trying to leap over the wall when there was really nothing on the other side.

I don't tell Zoe, but I've been online, too, reading more about what dolphins are like in the wild. How they stay with their families, sometimes forever, and they have whistle-names for each other.

✳ ✳ ✳ ✳ ✳ ✳

A few days go by without Zoe calling, and she stopped sending articles on DAT. Then this morning I get an email saying she hopes I'll be okay with her contacting the AquaPlanet people who rescued Nori. I don't answer.

A couple of hours later my phone rings.

"Hi, Zoe."

She launches right in. "After seeing where they are going to keep Nori, I thought you'd be with me on this."

"I'm not *against* you. I'm *for* my brother. What if it was your brother?"

"I'd feel the same. Therapy with dolphins is a hoax."

"Is it? What about therapy dogs?"

"Then have your stepfather buy him a dog. They've been domesticated. Dolphins are meant to be wild, and in an ocean."

"Zoe, what do you want from me? And how come

you're fixated on Nori, the one that might help Adam, instead of all the others?"

"I feel terrible for all of them, but it's probably too late for them. Nori's young and still has a chance at a normal dolphin life. She's the one we can help. They need to put her back with her mother before she forgets how to feed herself and be a wild dolphin."

"Just stop, Zoe! It's like you care more about Nori than you do about us being friends."

There's silence on the other end. "That's not true, Lily," she says finally. "I want us to be friends more than anything."

"Then prove it and stop talking about this. Nori's just one dolphin."

"Every dolphin should be free." Her voice is barely a whisper.

"Geez, Zoe, the world is full of—"

She cuts me off. "Maybe the reason I'm so upset about Nori is because I'm only one blind kid among millions of people who can't see, but not being blind would mean a lot to me. It would mean a normal life."

✳ ✳ ✳ ✳ ✳ ✳

I'm in the bathroom with Adam when Suzanne finds us. Day before yesterday, she finally moved Adam's potty to its new home on the floor next to the toilet.

"Hey, toots." She smiles at me. "How's our boy?"

"Adam, show Suzanne what you've learned."

He's through peeing, but still standing with his back arched. He doesn't look at me, or her.

"What have you learned, Adam?"

"You'll see." I cross my fingers, pull up his pants, then empty his potty into the toilet and flush. "Tell that pee-pee bye-bye."

Adam leans over and watches the water circle, then waves, but instead of turning his palm out, it's facing him.

She laughs. "What I'd give to be in his mind for a minute or two." She puts a stool in front of the sink for Adam to stand on to wash his hands.

"Can I ask you something?"

"Sure." She turns on the faucet and gives him a squirt of hand soap.

"How do you feel about them keeping N-O-R-I now that she's cured?"

She turns to look at me. "I think it's appalling."

"Do you? Do you really?"

"That poor animal belongs with her mother in the wild, not cooped up in the pen. But it's not my place to criticize your stepfather. He's my boss."

"He's totally behind this, isn't he?"

She turns to face me. "Not a word. Do you understand? He'd have every right to fire me."

I raise my right hand. "I promise, but he'd never fire you. He's totally dependent on you. So am I."

"No one is irreplaceable."

I think of my mother. "Some people are."

"The Oceanarium people can keep her as long as she's not cured, but they'll only keep her if she's healthy enough to go in with the other dol . . ." She dries Adam's hands with a towel. "D-o-l-p-h-i-n-s."

I try to rearrange what she's saying in my head, but I can't. "That doesn't make any sense."

"Ya think."

"They can keep her if she's still sick, but only if she's healthy?"

Adam jumps off the stool and runs down the hall.

Suzanne and I follow. She puts him in his high chair and hands him the Communicator 4.

Suzanne recorded the Communicator's responses so when Adam pushes the I WANT button, it sounds like Suzanne if she was an android. "Grapes."

"Good job, Adam." She gets grapes from the fridge, makes sure all the stems are removed, and puts them in a bowl.

Adam pushes I WANT again.

"Four, three, two, one." Suzanne counts like the therapists do at school to warn him she's taking the Communicator away, then puts the grapes on his tray. "Where were we?"

"N-O-R-I," I say.

"Right. Normally, a clean bill of health would mean she has to be returned to the Gulf, but they can keep her if she hasn't been cured of what brought her to them in the first place."

"But she has, hasn't she?"

"Yes and no. Her cancer is in 'remission.'" She makes quotation marks with her fingers.

I hold my hand up. "And remission can last a lifetime. So the truth is she's healthy, but by saying her cancer could return, Don's created the loophole that's letting them keep her."

"That's it."

"How do you know all this?"

"He told me. He's smug about it."

"Do you think it will help Adam?"

She shrugs. "It might help some. He's sure a happy little pea pod when he's with her."

I look at Adam. He takes a grape from the bowl and

places it on the tray in a line with the others. He is totally focused. "Do you think his happiness is worth keeping her in a tiny pen for her whole life?"

We both hear Don's car door slam.

Suzanne turns and busies herself at the sink.

I go to my room to email Zoe.

Please don't call AquaPlanet yet, okay? I'm thinking about it.

CHAPTER 25

Since my school let out for the summer, I've been going once a week to see how the Cutler Academy therapy program works so that we don't undo at home any progress he makes. Even though Adam's only been going for five weeks, Don's impatient with his progress or, in his opinion, lack of it. When Suzanne calls Friday to say she has jury duty on Monday, Don decides to take Adam to school himself. That scares me. If little boys making flowers upset him, watching Adam stacking two blocks or trying to match a red cup with the picture of a red cup is not going to build his confidence.

Don's always up before the sun, so when I come into the kitchen at seven thirty, he's already got a sleepy Adam in his high chair with a bowl of cereal in front of him. With his help getting Adam ready, we get to the school early enough for the morning singing circle, which I know exists only because we sometimes arrive in time to catch the end of the scratchy music.

Adam, as usual, runs to the microwave, which is on the counter, and stands on his tiptoes to look at his face reflected in the dark surface. The first time I saw him do this, I tried to think of another reflective surface in our house. Our microwave is above our stove. The mirrors are all farther above the ground than Adam is tall, and the only full-length mirror is on Don's closet wall. It makes me feel bad that he might not know what he looks like on the outside; none of us knows what he's like on the inside.

Adam holds the edge of the counter with his fingertips and puts his chin on his hands, totally absorbed in his reflection. I read somewhere that only humans, great apes, elephants, and dolphins have self-awareness and can recognize themselves in a mirror. Of course, scientists used to think tool use was the dividing line between humans and animals. They were wrong about that. Even birds use tools.

Each child has a small plastic chair with his or her picture Velcroed to the back. The other kids are already in their chairs. When Elisa calls his name, Adam runs to his and sits. I just have time to think, *so far so good*, when he jumps up and runs around the room, holding his arms out, before squeezing into Roberto's cubby. One of the teachers fetches him back to the circle.

Elisa puts on the music and the teachers start to sing along with a book of pictures: "Brown bear, brown bear, what do you see? I see a yellow duck, looking back at me."

As they go through the book, Don stands by the front door with his arms crossed over his chest like he can't commit to coming all the way into the room. My stomach's in a knot. If he pulls Adam out of this program that I think *is* helping, I'm not sure what I'll do. Leaving Adam's Saturdays with Nori as the only option would make any way Zoe and I might think of to send her home impossible.

Adam gets up again and runs into the cubicle where his plastic box of dolphins is on a shelf. Elisa goes to get him and signs *closed*, one palm up and the other hand perpendicular to it. Adam hops like a kangaroo over to the microwave, gazes at himself in its black surface, then goes to the window and looks out at the playground. The air conditioner under the window stirs his thin blond bangs. The morning light gives his face a soft glow. He reaches and touches the glass. I move so I can see what he sees, but there's no one there, just his reflection with me standing close behind him.

I'm not sure why Adam's fascination with his image upsets me. My first thought was Zoe and what it would mean to her if she could see herself, something she hasn't been able to do since she was four. But standing here behind Adam, I remember what Zoe said about Nori not being able to use her sonar in that first tank and that all she could see was wall, wall, wall. Mostly, I wonder what it means that Adam has started seeking out his own image.

"Time to do our numbers, Adam." Elisa smiles at Don. "He likes doing numbers."

Roberto has gotten up and is trudging around in circles, then pulls up a corner of the carpet and crawls under it. One of the teachers goes to get him.

Roberto's chair is next to Sonya's, the only little girl in the class. Adam comes over, peels Roberto's name off, and switches it with his own so his seat is now beside Sonya's.

A hint of a smile crosses Don's face.

"Good sitting, Adam," Elisa says.

Each kid has been handed a marker and an erasable board with ten squares. Elisa writes *1* in the first square on her own board and shows it to them. All attempt to write the numeral. Don walks over to where I'm standing behind Adam and watches him fill in the squares.

He gets one through four done, loses interest, and drops his board on the floor. He runs to a plastic bucket, takes out a ball, and throws it across the room. When it hits the wall, it begins to flash purple and red.

Elisa starts to get up.

"May I?" I've come often enough, I know what to do.

"Sure."

I retrieve the ball, get Adam's book with the Velcro strips, and peel off the picture of a ball. "Adam, do you want the ball?" I hand the picture to him. He doesn't look at it, but he knows the drill. He gives the picture to me and I give him the ball. "Good job," I say, like they say every time he does what he's supposed to do. I put the ball picture back in his book and put it on the desk. He throws the ball. It bounces off the sink and rolls under the lunch table. While I'm under the table, he goes to his book, takes off the ball picture, and brings it to me to trade. I look at Don. Whether he knows it or not, that's a huge step. Adam and I are communicating.

"Go check your schedules," Elisa calls out.

Adam goes straight to the room where his plastic box, containing three of his dolphins and a second copy of his *Little Dolphin* puppet book, is on a shelf. He points at it and jumps up and down. When no one takes it down for him, he crumples to the floor.

"Adam." Elisa stands him on his feet, but he lets his knees buckle. "Let's check your schedule." His feet drag along the carpet as she walks him to his strip of blue felt, which hangs with the others. His name and a picture Don took at Largo Center are at the top. In the picture, Adam is smiling. His hair is wet, and narrow streams of water snake from his bangs down his face. I can see the gray, new-moon curve of Squirt's snout pressed to his cheek, but the rest of the dolphin's head has been cropped out.

Under his name and picture is a vertical row of small Velcro circles, each of which has a picture attached to it. The other kids' schedules have different animals that match a table behind each partition, but Adam's is a dolphin. His pictures from top to bottom are chairs in a circle, a dolphin, the word *Play* above a pile of blocks, a picture of a toilet, and the word *Snack* above a glass of milk and a plate of cookies. Next is the word *Recess* with a drawing of a slide and a swing. The last is a picture of a car.

Elisa takes the dolphin picture and shows it to Adam. "Look, Adam, you're at the Dolphin Table." Her voice is full of excitement as though Disney World is waiting there.

Adam locks his wobbly knees, touches the picture, then runs behind the partition to the Dolphin Table.

"I'll work with Adam," Elisa says to one of the other teachers. To us she says, "Come watch."

Elisa puts an iPad in front of Adam. He turns it on and starts an animated dolphin story.

I look at Don. "He caught right on to it," I say.

Elisa gets out two small cubes, a cup, and a plate. "Okay, Adam, four, three, two, one. My turn." She takes the iPad from him and turns it screen-side down in her lap.

He looks at her, gets up, and hops toward the gap between the partition and the wall.

Elisa reaches behind her, catches his hand, and guides him back to his chair. She takes his hands and folds them in his lap. "Nice sitting."

Adam gets up and hops in a circle.

On the shelf next to his plastic box is a big exercise ball. This one is silver and has bumps on it. It looks like a space satellite. Elisa gets it down, pulls Adam's chair away from the table, and puts the ball in its place. "Adam, look at this." She bounces it with her hand. "Come sit here."

He runs to the ball, sits, and bounces.

"Nice sitting."

He reaches for the iPad.

"Work first." She places the cup, the plate, and two wooden blocks in front of Adam. "Can you stack these blocks?" She puts one on top of the other, then separates them.

Adam puts one on top of the other.

"Good job, Adam." She makes a mark on a paper in Adam's file. "Now can you hand me the cup?"

Adam stacks the blocks and bounces on the ball.

Elisa takes the cup, turns away from Adam, then turns back and puts the cup on the table. "Can you hand me the cup?"

He hands her a block and bounces.

This is repeated three more times before he finally hands her the cup. "Good job." She gives him the iPad.

He opens it to his video, lets the credits play, then restarts it. He does this until Elisa counts four, three, two, one, and takes it away from him.

I still don't know how he can he fail to do a simple behavior like hand Elisa a cup when he can use an iPad. I resist looking at Don.

Elisa has a handful of Skittles in a Ziploc. Adam loves Skittles. When he sees them, he signs *eat*.

Elisa puts the ball on the shelf and puts the little chair opposite hers at the desk. "Adam. Can you sit?" she asks.

He does.

"Good sitting."

He signs *eat*.

"Can you touch your nose?" To Don she says, "Asking them to touch their nose or an ear helps focus their attention."

Adam touches his nose, then signs *eat*.

"Adam, look at me."

Don stands in the corner, arms crossed, his face a mask, but his body language is another story. He doesn't have a clue about how progress is made or how slowly and methodically the therapists go, but he's judging them all the same.

"May I ask?" he says. "Why is eye contact so important?"

"Recent studies of autistic children show there seems to be a lag between what they see and what they hear. For them it's like watching a badly dubbed movie. If I can get the child to look at me and I speak slowly, it's less confusing."

"Thanks." He unfolds his arms and puts his hands in his pockets.

The knot in my stomach loosens.

"It was a good question." Elisa gets up and walks to the other side of the cubicle. "Come here." She crooks a finger. Adam gets up and walks to her. "Good job. High-five." She puts her hand up and so does Adam. He lets her touch his palm, but he's looking past her to the bag of Skittles on top of a file cabinet.

"Adam, look at me."

He shifts his eyes to hers, and I see something in my brother's face I've never seen before: confusion, panic, and pain. His brown eyes hold hers for as long as he can bear this deep a connection.

"Good, Adam. Can you sit?" Elisa says, just in time.

He whirls and plunges into his chair.

"Good job." She gives him a Skittle.

I glance at Don but can't tell if he saw the same thing. There's no change in his expression, which makes me doubt my own eyes. Maybe the ache I feel in my chest is because I wish more than anything that Adam could connect, and painlessly.

"The system we use is the same as B. F. Skinner used," Elisa says.

"To train animals," Don says.

Elisa studies him for a second. "The system of rewards is very effective."

Don's brow creases. He's the one in pain now.

CHAPTER 26

Finally, after five Saturdays, the parking attendant at the Oceanarium recognizes Don, rips a ticket in half, and wishes us a good day. It's just me, Don, and Adam. Suzanne took the day off and I didn't ask Zoe.

"Hello, hello." We get the usual overly enthusiastic, two-handed wave from Sandi when we come through the glass doors. There's the bucket of fish on the dock, and Nori's at the edge of the raft with her mouth open.

Usually we're the only ones here, but today a mom, dad, and two kids, all in black-and-blue wet suits, are knee-deep in the water with two dolphins. Adam runs right toward Nori's pool. Don follows. I stop to watch the family.

Two dolphins have been moved from their pens to the unfenced half of the lagoon. The little girl sits in the water, and one of the dolphins puts its head on her legs.

She leans and kisses its beak. It's a sweet picture like the ones on the Oceanarium's website.

At the far end of the lagoon opposite where the family is standing, an employee holds a long pole with a tennis ball duct-taped to the end. She blows a whistle, lifts the pole, then hits the water with the ball. The little girl's brother points to the second dolphin, then at the girl with the pole. The dolphin zips away and a moment later leaps out of the water at the point where the tennis ball hits the water. The boy's parents applaud his dolphin-training technique.

I look over at my brother. He's on his stomach on the dock, arms outstretched to Nori. Another perfect picture: a cute little blond kid having the time of his life. Snapshots. That's what Don calls the pictures in our albums at home: moments in time that supposedly capture the heart of what's going on. But there's no way to tell if the smiles are real or artificial. I can't help but wonder how many dolphin lives would have been saved if the line of their jaws turned down instead of up.

Now that Don has seen how structured Adam's life is at school, I don't see why it's not as obvious to him as it is to me that this is nothing more than a weekly swim with Nori. Sandi's focus is trying to get him to talk because she knows that's what Don wants. For the hour and a half we're here, she tries to get him to say *Nori* over and over until I want to scream. But there are no consequences when he doesn't. He gets to swim with her no matter what. And worse, they've turned Nori into a robot. Instead of Adam being special to her, someone she loves to see, now, after she drags him around the pool attached to her dorsal fin, or swims away when Adam points, she heads straight back to the raft for a fish.

Sandi's in the water to make sure Adam's hand is properly positioned around the base of Nori's dorsal fin. Don looks over and smiles at me.

I can't force a smile. I leave instead.

There's a pizza stand and a few picnic tables near the killer whale show tank. The tables have umbrellas. I go sit at one and call Zoe. A flock of white ibis are probing the grass under the tables. They and the pigeons are the luckiest animals in this place.

"Hey. Where are you?" Zoe says.

"Same place I am every Saturday."

Behind me, a metal door goes up.

"What was that?" Zoe says.

"They're letting people into the killer whale show."

"Are you going?"

"No. We'll be home about two. Want to come swim?"

"Sure. Or you could come over here and we could try to call AquaPlanet."

"Stop it, Zoe."

The second of the two metal doors goes up. "I've changed my mind. I'm going to the show. I'll call you later."

It's twelve thirty and blistering hot as people start into the killer whale show. Only the top six rows of the twelve that encircle the tank are roofed. I climb to the very top row where there's shade and a breeze. From this height, I can see that this tank is all there is. There's no place else for the orca or the three Pacific white-sided dolphins to be.

The tank is shaped like a vase, round and swollen at one end, narrow at the neck, and wide at the mouth. It's the same shape as the paper vase Daniel and Roberto pasted over their flowers, the same shape as some of vases we have under the sink at home, left over from flowers delivered after Mom died.

A girl in a black-and-white wet suit is standing in the shade of an umbrella behind the short wall at the top of the tank. It's so shallow at that end that Carlotta, their orca, is resting with her tail against the bottom of the pool, mouth open. When the girl hears the click of a microphone being turned on, she picks up and carries two buckets of fish through a gate that opens onto a long, narrow raft. Carlotta makes a tight turn and follows her.

A booming voice like a radio announcer's welcomes us to the Bayside Oceanarium's Killer Whale Show; then the volume of the music is turned up. Two more trainers run over the bridge and out onto the dock. They wave to the audience with both hands.

Carlotta positions herself in front of the first trainer. The three Pacific white-sided dolphins line up in front of the other two trainers, mouths open. The music softens and the other girl trainer shouts out the second welcome.

"The Bayside Oceanarium was built in 1955 and is the longest-operating aquarium in the United States. It was the first to exhibit a killer whale, and remains the only aquarium with a killer whale in an exhibit with Pacific white-sided dolphins, one of the world's smallest and fastest dolphins. They are capable of doing twenty-five miles an hour in the open ocean."

"Where they oughta be." I don't realize I've said this out loud until the people in front of me glance around. I'm more surprised that it just popped out. It's like I'm channeling Zoe.

"Carlotta has been the star of this show since 1970 . . ."

I do the math and gasp. *Forty-four years!* It can't be the same orca. Maybe they name each new one Carlotta like they do replacement Flippers.

"She is twenty feet long and weighs seven thousand pounds. We keep the seawater chilled to a comfortable fifty degrees—comfortable for her, anyway." The girl hugs herself like she's cold.

The show starts with the white-sided dolphins doing synchronized somersaults. While they perform, the first trainer occupies Carlotta by giving her small pieces of fish that I imagine must be as satisfying as a tadpole to an alligator.

The male trainer gets in the water and does the backstroke while one of the dolphins swims alongside him on its back. He keeps a close eye on Carlotta. I wonder if it's because the orca at SeaWorld in Orlando killed his trainer.

It's time for Carlotta to earn bigger fish. The music switches to Enrique Iglesias's "Don't Turn Off the Lights," and the trainers clap in time, encouraging the audience to do the same.

Carlotta turns on her side, raises a huge paddle-like flipper. Her trainer steps aboard and rides her around the tank. Both she and Carlotta wave at the audience, then Carlotta delivers her back to the raft and she steps off.

Carlotta dives, and when she surfaces again, one of the other trainers is riding on her head. Carlotta brings her to the raft, then opens her mouth. Large chunks of fish are fed into it.

I shouldn't have come to this show and definitely shouldn't have climbed all the way to the top. There's no escape without the entire audience seeing me. If I had Zoe's guts, I'd do just that—walk out. But I don't. I stay there watching them degrade this poor whale.

Carlotta turns on her back; her trainer steps onto her stomach and is carried around the perimeter of the pool to be delivered back to the raft. Carlotta dives, shoots out of the water, and splashes back in, sending gallons of icy water over the wall to drench the people sitting in the splash zone.

For her last act, Carlotta launches herself onto the raft and lies there with one trainer on her back and the other two on either side, smiling like she's their trophy.

I stay and watch people file out the gate until they're all gone, then I hear the clatter of the far metal door being lowered. A few teenage boys in Oceanarium uniforms race each other to the top row of bleachers on the opposite side of the pool. They holler, curse each other, and the winner whoops. Then they search the bleachers for any trash left behind. I watch for quite a while before my cell phone ringing draws the attention of the trainer who's feeding the last of the fish to the dolphins and Carlotta.

"You gotta leave, miss."

I look at my phone. It's Don. "Yeah."

"Where are you?"

"In the killer whale show."

"Sorry if it's not over, but your brother's ready to go."

"Okay."

I sit for a minute more watching Carlotta. All the fish are gone and she's lying in the water. Just lying there in her vase.

"Miss?"

"I'm leaving." I stand, and while he watches me, I text Zoe. *2 @ your house. Let's get Nori back to her mom.*

CHAPTER 27

I easily find Zoe's house on Tigertail, a few blocks up from the park where we met. It's an old Grove house like ours, though hers is wooden instead of coral rock. Her mom answers the door. I glance around quickly as she leads me through the sparsely furnished living room. Most of the furniture is pushed against the wall except for one chair and a footstool near the center of the room.

"Sorry. It always looks like this. Zoe has me shift a piece of furniture every day so she can practice echolocation."

"I still don't know how she does it. I tried and could only tell my wall from an open doorway because I peeked."

"She's determined to be—"

"I know, the greatest blind kid ever."

When her mother smiles at me, I see in her eyes the same pain I see nearly every time Don looks at Adam.

Zoe's at her desk. A mechanical, nasal-sounding

male voice reads the computer page so fast, and in such detail, I don't know how she can keep up. And it reads everything on the page. "h t t p colon backslash backslash w w w dot aqua planet backslash contact us backslash reservations backslash p h p."

"That voice is awful. How do you stand it?"

"He does make me wish I could see."

Once again, I've jammed my foot in my mouth. "I'm sorry."

"Don't worry. I've gotten used to him. I imagine he's very handsome and has a really nice car."

The keyboard Zoe's using looks like mine except that all the letters and numbers have bumps on them. Skype is open on the screen.

The voice says, "Toll free one dash eight six six dash five five five dash two four one nine."

"Is Mom gone?" she whispers.

I look over my shoulder. "Uh-huh."

"Good. Close the door, will you." She listens to me cross the room and waits for the lock to click. "Dial number," she says.

Skype makes its little bubble-popping sound as it dials.

My heart is pounding. We should have practiced what we would say.

"We're sorry, our reservation desk is closed." It's their answering machine. "Please leave a number and we will call you back during business hours."

"Hang up," Zoe instructs Skype. "Let's decide what message to leave, then call back."

"Just say we have news about Nori. And leave this number. I don't want them calling our house when Don's home."

I call Zoe the next day. "Hi." She sounds bummed.

"They didn't call, did they?"

"No, they didn't, and Mom said not to try again."

"How come?"

"She says it's not our call to make. Your stepfather has to make that decision."

I took forever to make up my mind about this, and now I'm not going to give up. "I'm not willing to leave it up to Don. Are you?"

The smile returns to Zoe's voice. "Of course not."

"Good. If we don't hear from AquaPlanet in a day or two, we'll try again."

"It won't work unless your stepfather's onboard."

"I know," I say, but I'm not sure what to do about that.

CHAPTER 28

I stand outside Don's bedroom door trying to decide how to go about this. How to make him see beyond Sandi's phony efforts and how wrong it is to keep Nori in a pen for Adam's sake when she should be returned to her family. All this is running through my mind when Don opens his door. We both jump.

"I was just about to knock. Can we talk?"

Past him, on his bedside table, is a picture of my mother taken on their honeymoon in Cancun.

"I'm in kind of a rush. Can you tell me while I fix some toast?" He starts to close his door.

"It's nice that you still have Mom's picture on your table."

He glances over his shoulder. When he turns to me again, his lips are compressed. "It's not just that I miss her. It's how I keep her alive. I can look at her face and remember our lives together, the laughs we had, the special moments. I'm afraid without it there for me to look at every night, I'll start to forget."

"I feel the same way."

I can tell he doesn't know what more to say. He nods and starts for the kitchen. "So what's on your mind?"

"You didn't know Mom when we had William Penn, did you?"

"I guess not. Who was he?" He takes two slices of bread from the bag and puts them in the toaster oven, then brings the bag to his mouth, sucks the air out, and spins it to keep the air from getting back in. He thinks it keeps the bread fresher longer.

"He was our Quaker parakeet."

"Lily, is this a long story? I really have to get to the hospital."

"It's an important story."

"Okay." He opens the fridge, looking for the butter.

"It's on the counter."

"What is?"

"The butter."

"Thanks. Tell me about William Penn. Cute name. A Quaker parakeet named after the Quaker founder of Pennsylvania."

"Mom found him on the ground near the pond in front of Baptist Hospital. Lots of them nest in the trees there."

"I know. There are huge, noisy flocks of them."

"Mom and I hand raised him. He was so tame, he'd lie on his back in the palm of my hand and let me tickle his stomach."

The bell on the toaster oven rings.

I talk faster. "I loved him, but Mom said it wasn't fair to keep him shut in a cage for the rest of his life."

Don's sitting at the center island counter, chewing his toast and looking at me. He gets where I'm going with this. I can see it in his eyes.

"It's not the same thing, Lily."

"It's worse!" I lower my voice. "I'm afraid if we keep Nori much longer, she'll forget how to be a wild dolphin; she'll forget her family and her family will forget her."

"Wouldn't that be a good thing? It hurts to remember."

Mom's picture on Don's nightstand comes to mind. And her driver's license, which I keep in my desk drawer. We're both keeping her alive in our memories. "If you think forgetting is a good thing, why do you keep Mom's picture by your bed?"

I can see that stings. He closes his eyes. "You have a point, okay, but as long as Nori is helping your brother . . ."

"Helping him do what? He was already a good swimmer." I take a deep breath to stay calm. "And just because he's happy when he's with her isn't enough reason to keep her in that chlorinated lagoon for the rest of her life."

"I think it is."

"I don't. And Mom wouldn't, either."

"Because she let a bird go?" He gets up and carries his plate to the sink.

"Because it was the right thing to do. We took William Penn to the pond every afternoon. He stuck really close to us at first, but after a while, he'd fly up in the trees with the other birds. If one got too close, he'd fly back and land on my head." I dampen the sponge and wipe up the crumbs Don left by the sink. "I really thought William Penn loved me as much as I loved him and that he'd never leave, but Mom said to give him time. She was right. One day we got ready to leave and he didn't follow us to the car. Mom told me it was time to tell him good-bye—that he was ready to be a wild bird again. I cried like I'd lost my best friend. Mom put her arms around me and her forehead against mine and said she knew I loved him and that he loved me, but we had to choose what was best for him, not for us."

Don's back is to me. "Nori makes your brother happy." He squirts some soap on his plate and turns on the water.

"Yeah. For short periods of time. Mom said the creatures of this earth are here for their own sake."

He turns from the sink. "That was before her son was diagnosed with autism."

I shake my head. "Remember what that woman at the Largo Center said? Adam is an autistic child and he will be an autistic adult. A dolphin's not going to change that."

"Maybe not, but he may have a happier life because of Nori."

"That still doesn't make keeping her right." Don senses I'm running out of steam and gets that smirky look on his face, which makes me mad. "It's okay that our lives revolve around Adam, but we can make sure Nori doesn't spend her life circling a pen the size of our swimming pool because of him. Please, Dad—" I realize what I said and feel my face go hot. I don't know where that came from. I've never thought of him as my father. "Sorry. I mean Don."

His eyes soften. "Why are you sorry?"

I shrug. "I'm not the one you wanted to hear that from."

He wads up his paper napkin and puts it in the trash can under the sink, then stands for a moment looking out at the backyard. "You're wrong."

"About which thing?"

"About not wanting to hear you call me Dad."

"Am I?"

He turns. "I thought it was too much to hope for." He holds his arms out, and I walk into them. He kisses the top of my head.

"What about Nori?"

"I'll think about it."

PART IV

CHAPTER 29

Nori lies in water so crystal clear it stings. All day long she stays near the fence that divides her pen from the dolphin they call Rosa. Rosa is older than the dolphins in the other pens; she reminds Nori of her mother.

The scrape on Nori's beak where she tried to swim through the fencing on the first day is healing. She heard the other dolphins and tried to join them. The moment they lifted her off the truck in the canvas sling and placed her in the water, she took off and hit the fence at nearly full speed. At least the dolphins can talk to each other here, and Nori now believes this is as good as it's ever going to get for any of them. She tries to be grateful to be out of that other place where her sonar bounced back at her from all directions, and for the little human who comes once a week.

The other dolphins are kept so that families of humans can pet them and pretend to train them. For that hour every day, they're allowed in the open, fence-free side of the lagoon, where they can race each other back and forth, soar into the air, and do somersaults like free dolphins. But to get fed, they must perform for the humans.

Nori's only job is to play with the little boy they call Adam. Though all the days of the week run together for Nori, she knows when he's coming because they don't feed her until he's there. They must think she wouldn't be as willing to play if she wasn't hungry, but his visit is the only fun she has. It reminds her of being with her mother in the murky, warm waters of the Gulf, and the children who came to visit them there.

There's a canopy in the center of the lagoon. As the sun moves across the sky, the dolphins, in their individual pens, try to stay in the shadow it casts. By now, the sun has crossed and Nori's pool is completely exposed. Still she lies on the surface, beside Rosa. They listen to the loud music, and the shrieks and laughter of children from the other side of the tall fence, and Nori waits for Saturday to come.

CHAPTER 30

Zoe's coming over to swim at three, so against all my natural instincts, I start cleaning my room. I don't want her measuring and memorizing this obstacle course. I'm so into it that when Don raps on my door, I nearly jump out of my skin.

"What?"

He looks at my made bed and the path I've cleared of clothes. He smiles. "I hate to interrupt this miracle, but we need to pick Adam up from school. Suzanne went home sick."

"Zoe's coming at three."

"We'll be back." He turns and heads down the hall.

"Why do I have to go?"

No answer.

*   *   *   *   *   *

From the Cutler Academy, Don drives up Red Road through all the school zones instead of cutting over on 88th Street to Old Cutler Road.

"Why are you going this way?"

Don looks at me in the rearview mirror. "Nails and haircut."

"No wonder Suzanne got sick."

Don's eyes crinkle into a smile.

The barbershop is in a little shopping center off Sunset Drive. When Don pulls into a space in front, Adam leans his head against the window and watches the barber pole turning. He always reacts to having his hair cut like it's being yanked out strand by bloody strand, but he loves watching the barber pole. His eyes follow it until we cross the threshold. Both barbers and the manicurist turn when we come in. Adam is their worst nightmare, and Don pays them big-time to take him.

Don puts Adam in the chair; Adam exits it like a slinky. Don catches him and puts him back in the chair; Adam starts to kick and scream.

There's a cute guy about fifteen or sixteen in the second chair getting his nails done while the other barber cuts his hair. He glanced at me when we came in, but now all eyes are on Adam.

It occurs to me for the first time that I'll probably never have a boyfriend and no one will ever want to marry me. I'll spend my life as Adam's sister, a carrier of the autism gene, if there is such a thing. I turn and face the parking lot in case tears come.

Adam is shrieking, kicking his legs, and rocking from side to side. When I turn around, I see the manicurist look at the kid and roll her eyes. I glare at her, and she looks away.

"I have an idea," I say, but over Adam's screams, no one hears me. I say it louder.

"What?" Don snaps.

"Cut his hair out where he can see the barber pole."

The manicurist gives a short, sharp laugh, and the kid grins at her. I hate him, and her.

Don snatches Adam out of the chair and carries him outside. As soon as Adam realizes he's won, he stops screaming. Don holds him up so he can see the barber pole turning. He's instantly mesmerized.

The barber follows with his comb and scissors. There's a stool by the door with a dead potted plant on it. I put the plant on the floor and carry the stool outside. Don starts to put Adam on it, then decides it's better to sit on it himself and balance Adam on his knee. The barber goes right to work, and Adam is oblivious.

His little legs bounce, and he's jabbering to himself, but is otherwise unaware his hair is cascading to the walkway except what clings to Don's pants.

There's a cheese shop two doors down. People going in and out smile at us, like we're a normal family.

"I can't imagine why we never thought of this before." Don smiles at me.

We? I think, but don't say so. "What about his nails?"

"Take his shoes off and see how he reacts."

I do. Adam ignores me, but his legs swing back and forth. His toenails are too long for him to wear any shoes except open-toed sandals. His fingernails are lethal weapons.

The barber glances inside at the manicurist and sees she's still doing the same hand. She's smiling and giggling. The barber turns to me. "Tell Sherry to get out here." His tone is sharp, and I should wonder who he thinks he's talking to, but I'm also used to feeling desperate to get something involving Adam over with. Instead I smile. I know trimming Adam's nails terrifies her, and she deserves it.

Sherry glances at me when she wheels her little stool out. I imagine she and that boy were laughing at Adam, so I don't smile or anything.

"Will you hold his foot?" Sherry says to me.

"I'll do it," Don says.

Adam's haircut is over, so Don shifts him from his knee to his lap and pins one leg at a time to his long thigh. Adam leans his head back against Don's chest, stares up at the barber pole, and swings his free leg. Don puts his chin on the top of Adam's head.

This is when I forgive Don everything. It's pitiful to see how much he loves his son and has to pretend in a quiet moment that Adam feels it, too, because he doesn't wiggle free or scream.

The toenails get clipped pretty easily, but about the time Sherry starts on the nails on his right hand, a car goes by with its woofers pounding. Adam yanks his hand away, covers his ears, screws his face up, and starts to cry.

"That's it," Don says. "We'll do the other hand when he's asleep."

Sherry couldn't look more relieved. Her hands actually shook as she worked, knowing if she cut him he'd flip out.

Don pays while I get Adam in the car. It's two thirty.

Don drives two blocks and turns left. Not toward home.

"Now where?"

"We need milk and eggs. I'll stop at Publix, and you can run in."

He finds a parking place in the shade, and rolls down the windows. "Take Adam with you. I need to make a couple of calls."

I don't bother arguing. It's quicker just to get it over with. Adam's harness is at home, so I carry him across the parking lot and into the store. The carts are near the customer service desk, where a girl with Down syndrome is standing with both pockets of her sweatpants pulled inside out. "I had a five-dollar bill," she says.

"I'm sorry," the customer service lady says. "No one has turned it in."

I put Adam in the child's seat of a cart and fasten the seat belt.

"I'm not supposed to lose money." The girl crosses her arms on the counter and puts her forehead down.

I turn my back, pull the money Don handed me from my pocket, and take a crumpled five from the wad. "Excuse me," I say to the customer service lady, "I just found this on the floor." I hand the five over the top of the girl's head.

The woman's brow crinkles in disbelief at the chances of the girl's money being found, then figures it out and smiles. "Miss." She pats the girl's elbow. "This young lady has found your money."

The girl lifts her head, looks at the five-dollar bill, then turns and throws her arms around me.

✳ ✳ ✳ ✳ ✳ ✳

Eggs and dairy are at the back of the store. I'm feeling like a kind and thoughtful person as I wheel my brother down the aisle.

There's an old lady standing in front of the organic, cage-free brown eggs. She leans over her walker and holds a magnifying glass to each price tag. Her hearing aid is whistling. It must sound a little like a dolphin whistle to Adam because he imitates it. I steer the cart over to get milk first.

I come back with the milk, and she's still inspecting the prices. When she leans toward the next one down the line, she passes gas. I stifle a giggle. Adam imitates the sound, which sounds like the raspberry Nori makes.

"Shhhh." I put my finger to my lips.

Another lady walks up, smiles at Adam, and takes a carton of eggs.

The old lady farts again, louder this time. Adam mimics the sound, then leans his head back against my chest and says, "Noisy bottom."

The woman with the carton of eggs bursts out laughing; so do I, then gasp. "Adam. Oh, my god." I undo the seat belt, pick him up, hug him tightly, and run down the aisle and out the front door of the store.

Don jumps and his cell phone pops out of his hand and drops between the seats when I shout, "Guess what!"

"Jesus, you scared me—"

I'm grinning from ear to ear.

"What?"

"Adam spoke."

"What? No." Tears swim in his eyes. "What did he say?"

I remember Don's wish to hear Adam call him Daddy, but I can't help myself, I start to laugh. "An old lady over by the eggs farted, and he . . . said—" I'm laughing so hard I can't catch my breath.

Adam creates another raspberry and says, "Noisy bottom."

A tear runs down Don's cheek. He swipes at it and starts to laugh—a laugh as full of joy as a laugh can be. He opens the car door, takes Adam from me, and lifts him into the air.

Adam does another raspberry, then swings his arms like a swimmer and giggles.

"It's the dolphin." Don beams. "I told you."

Happiness turns to a lump in my throat.

CHAPTER 31

On the drive home from Publix, my cell phone rings. It's Zoe. "I thought you were going to call and tell her we're running late," I say to Don before answering.

"I did."

"Hi, Zoe."

"Where are you?"

"We're almost home."

"Can you come here instead? I want to teach you to play backgammon."

Backgammon? "Sure. I guess. Can you drop me at Zoe's?" I say to Don.

* * * * * *

Zoe's at her desk. There's a backgammon board open on her bed. "Mom, are you still here?" Zoe says.

"She's gone."

"Good. Close the door."

I check the hallway, then shut the door. "Backgammon?"

"Sure. After we call AquaPlanet." She maximizes the Skype screen.

"What about your mother? Want to use my phone so you don't get in trouble?"

"Don't worry about me. You're stepfather is wrong and so is Mom. Nori can't wait for our parents to see we're right about this."

She's puts it on speaker so I can listen, and lowers her voice, trying to sound like an adult. I cover my mouth to muffle a giggle.

"Good afternoon. AquaPlanet." It's a young guy's voice. "How may I direct your call?"

"This is Dr. Moran's assistant. He's been treating a dolphin at the Bayside Oceanarium. I believe her name— let me see." Zoe noisily fans a few pages in a book on her desk. "Here it is. Nori. She's doing beautifully, and we'd like to schedule a release date. I'm sure we'd all like to see her back with her mother and the rest of her pod."

"I'm sorry. I just schedule trips. Could you call back later this afternoon? The owner is out with a group now."

"This is my third attempt to reach him." Zoe's voice drops lower. "I could give you our number here at the office and perhaps he could call when it's convenient for him."

"Okay. Sure."

Now what? I think, but Zoe gives him her cell number. She thinks so much quicker on her feet than I do. Her cell has a voice that tells her who's calling.

"You know what?" the guy says. "I'm pretty sure Nori's mother is dead."

"No!" we say in unison. Tears swim in my eyes. "That can't be," I whisper. The world can't be that unfair.

Zoe reaches over, finds my hand, and holds it. "What happened?" she says in her own voice.

He doesn't seem to notice. "If it's the one I'm thinking about, she ingested fishing line, hook and all. That happens pretty often. People feed the dolphins and they get used to following fishing boats, then they graduate from taking fish scraps tossed overboard to snatching fish being reeled in. They get really good at it, leaving just the head and the hook. If they take the entire fish, fisherman usually cut the line." His voice fades like he's walked away from the phone.

"Hello?" Zoe says.

"I'm here." His voice returns, unexpectedly loud. We both jump.

We hear a buzzer like when someone enters or leaves

a convenience store. "Hang on. I'll be right with you," the kid says to whoever came in, then to Zoe, "We name all dolphins that visit our boats, and I was looking for the list. We keep records of any found dead and of unexplained disappearances."

We wait.

"Sorry," he says. "Still looking."

I hold my breath.

"That's funny," he says.

"What is?"

"She never had a name. She's on the list as Nori's mom. Found dead August 3, Shell Island. Fishing line, hook, and lure."

"Thank you." Zoe's voice is a whisper. "I'll let Dr. Moran know."

"The others will be happy to know Nori's doing well." There's a click and a dial tone, but Zoe just sits there.

I finally tell the JAWS program to end the call.

"Now what?" Zoe says.

"I don't know." I think about it for a minute and say, "I'm not going to tell Don. The Gulf is where she came from, and she must still have family there. Aunts and cousins."

"Do you think it would be the same?"

"I live with my stepfather. So, no, not the same, but better than the alternative."

CHAPTER 32

I know it's impossible—Adam's four and a half—but I swear he knows when I'm least able to take one of his tantrums. The minute I put him in his high chair this morning, he starts to cry and twist in his seat. My stomach knots. I know what's coming.

"Please don't, Adam. Not today."

I hurry to put his bowl of Cheerios on his tray. He grabs it, pitches it to the floor, then screws up his face and starts to scream.

The door to Don's office flies open and he marches across the living room to the kitchen. "What happened?"

"You always think there's an answer to that, don't you?" I'm trying not to cry.

"Where's Suzanne?"

"It's only seven. She's not here yet."

His expression softens and, by the way he looks at me, I know he's as aware of what today is as I am.

He starts to touch my shoulder, but doesn't. "Go on. I'll deal with him and clean up."

"Thanks." I blot my eyes on the dish towel.

Of course, Don's idea of dealing with him is to put him in the padded play yard and leave him to scream himself hoarse.

I escape to my room, take my mother's driver's license from the drawer under my computer, and crawl into bed to stare at her face. There are other, better pictures of her in the house, but I like this one. She'd just renewed it that February and hated the picture, complaining that she needed a haircut and the woman had taken it before she smiled. I don't think I could stand it if she'd been smiling. Her license was only five months old when she was killed two years ago today. There's something about it being good for another eight years that makes her dying even more unfair.

Every so often, I creep down the hall to check on Adam. This time he's standing, jerking on the sides of his play yard and shrieking, sirenlike. I put on his dolphin DVD, but he doesn't see it or me. For a moment, I envy how free he is to vent his unhappiness and frustration. I wonder what he'd do if I crawled in there with him and screamed my head off.

* * * * * *

I couldn't sleep last night. I lay in bed thinking about my mom and how, now that Nori's mother is dead, there may not be a home for Nori to return to.

Adam rarely sleeps through the night, and twice, before I finally fell asleep, I heard him babbling to himself, squeaking, then giggling. Maybe Nori's mom dying and how happy Adam is with her is the world telling me to butt out.

By the time I wake this morning, it's nearly ten. Don's gone to the hospital; Suzanne's fed Adam and is bathing him.

"Hey, toots." Suzanne smiles, then her lips compress. "Don left an article for you. It's on the kitchen counter."

"What kind of article?"

"Something he downloaded off the Internet."

"Have you read it?"

"Some of it."

"And?"

"They're finding a lot of sick dolphins in the Gulf."

Suzanne forgets to spell *dolphin*. Adam squeaks, rolls on his belly in the tub, puts his face in the water and blows raspberries, then kicks water all over her and the floor.

Lily, read this is scrawled in Don's terrible handwriting.

Bottlenose dolphins in Louisiana's Barataria Bay, which was heavily oiled after the BP Deepwater Horizon spill, have lung damage and adrenal hormone abnormalities, according to a study published in the Journal of Environmental Science & Technology. This is the first evidence of dolphins exhibiting injuries consistent with toxic effects of exposure to petroleum hydrocarbons. The study concludes that the health effects are significant and likely will lead to reduced survival and ability to reproduce. The increase in the number of dolphin strandings now includes more than 1,050 animals that have stranded along the Gulf Coast from the Texas/Louisiana border through Franklin County, FL.

These findings are in contrast to dolphins sampled in Sarasota Bay, FL, an area not affected by the oil spill. Dr. Lori Schwacke, the study's lead author, says, "I've never seen such a high prevalence of very sick animals."

Don underlined *Franklin County, FL.* I carry the article to my room and turn on my computer and pull up a map. Panama City, Florida—where Nori came from—is located in the toxic area.

Nori's mother is dead, and her pod of relatives is in the toxic waters off the northern Gulf Coast. This is just the ammunition Don needs to make a case for keeping her. Even worse, it leaves Zoe and me with no other option.

The decapitated doll's head watches as I fling myself across my bed. I sob and can't stop, so I fuel it by thinking about my own mom. I picture her behind the wheel while the fire department uses the Jaws of Life to try to get her out in time. I only imagine this; I don't really know what happened because Don won't tell me, but in my mind she was still alive and frightened. I cry harder. When I feel myself letting go of Momma, I cry for William Penn, and then because my best friend doesn't even know what I look like.

"Are you okay?" Suzanne's in the doorway, holding Adam, who's wrapped in a towel.

I sit up. "We're never going to get you-know-who out of there."

"Sure we are."

I suddenly hate her perpetual optimism.

"How?" I snap.

"I don't know that yet, but we're not leaving N-O-R-I in that place."

Adam flaps his hand.

"Did you see that?"

"I did. He can copy his name at school. Right, big boy?" She jiggles him.

"N-O-R-I," I spell.

Adam squeaks.

"That's impossible."

"Maybe not," Suzanne says. "I don't think we have a clue what he understands."

CHAPTER 33

This Saturday a trainer has joined Sandi, who sits on the dock with Adam. Sandi tries to get Adam to copy the hand signals the trainer gives Nori, and Nori tries to do what's asked of her. The trainer wants her to bring Adam a beach ball being blown around the pool by a breeze. Nori doesn't get the ball thing, but swims away when the trainer signals her, then swims back and opens her mouth for a piece of fish, which she doesn't get because she didn't bring the ball.

Adam wants in the water with Nori, but he's being held in place by Sandi's grip on the back strap of his life jacket. She keeps glancing at us and smiling like everything is going as well as can be expected. I think she's desperate to prove this is helping him or she'll be out of a job again. I'm rooting for a meltdown.

Don, Suzanne, and I sit on the bench—watching. I'm picking my cuticles.

Suzanne nudges me. "Go on. I'll stay here with Adam."

I take my cell phone from my pocket and look at the time. It's 10:25. The upper-deck dolphin show starts in fifteen minutes.

Before I knew about Nori's mom, or how toxic the waters she came from are, I had this idea to take Don to see the upper-deck show. I thought if he saw how poorly the dolphins are treated, he'd change his mind about helping them keep Nori. Suzanne agreed. Now, as pointless as it seems, I'm sticking to the plan for lack of a better one. Zoe and I hoped to have a place for her to go before we talked Don into releasing her. Now the plan is to talk him into it, then find a place for her to go.

Adam is squirming and twisting, trying to get away from Sandi. He flaps his hand at Nori, who comes and presses her beak against his foot. Adam giggles and puts his arms out.

Adam spoke in Publix and hasn't said another word. Knowing it happened has perked up Sandi's efforts. She holds him in place. "Adam, can you say 'Nori'?"

He screams and kicks his feet.

I smile to myself and wonder how much would be accomplished if Don and Sandi—a pair of control freaks—left Nori and Adam to their own devices.

Don puts his head back and sighs.

Suzanne pats his arm. "You've never seen the rest of this place. Why don't you and Lily take a walk? I'll keep an eye on things here."

Don closes his eyes for a second, nods, then puts both hands on his knees and gets up. "Thanks." He smiles at me. "I'd like that."

"One of the shows starts in a few minutes. Want to go there?"

"Sure."

I glance back at Suzanne after we go through the glass doors into the lobby. She holds up crossed fingers.

Don's quiet as we walk toward the show tank.

"You want to see the stingrays?" I say.

"Not really."

When we get to the dark, echoey tunnel with its row of windows—a submarine view of a concrete tank—Don turns to go up the stairs. I want him to see how barren the dolphin's tank is: no sand, no seaweed, no fish, nothing except six circling dolphins and three big pipes, but I don't want to give him a chance to say no. "Come this way first." I pull him by his sleeve to the center window, which has the best view of the three big pipes.

Dolphin after dolphin sweeps by the windows. Don

watches for a minute, then turns toward the stairs. I follow.

Upstairs, it's broiling hot. Don heads straight up to stand in the shade of the awning.

The girl trainers aren't in the bow of the pirate ship yet. When the first one arrives, the dolphins all stop circling and gather beneath the bow—heads out of the water, mouths open.

Exactly like the show weeks ago, the girl wearing the microphone shouts out a welcome. Kiss's "Rock and Roll All Nite" blares, and the girls signal the dolphins. They all lift out of the water, tail-walk backward across the pool, dive, and race back to get fed.

I glance at Don. His expression is blank, which is better than if he was smiling.

The dolphins do all the same tricks, then comes the trivia game. The questions are the same, and when the trainer declares the dolphins the winners, she high-fives the girl next to her exactly like last time.

They turn the music down, and the girl introduces each dolphin and tells how they are all moms and what a lucky boy Troy is.

When this doesn't get a reaction from Don, I can't stand it anymore. "I wonder where their babies are?"

"I'm sure they sell them to other aquariums."

He knows and doesn't care. "Don't you think that's awful?"

He looks at me. "I'm hungry. Want something to eat?"

"No, thanks."

On the way back out we stop at a food kiosk, and Don gets a slice of pepperoni pizza and bottle of water. "Sure you don't want anything?"

"I'm sure." I shake my head, but my stomach has a vote of its own and growls loudly. Don smiles and orders a second slice.

We sit at one of the metal picnic tables. "The killer whale show is next. You want to go there?" I ask.

"If you do, but I've seen enough."

It hasn't worked. He's seen how the dolphins live and he doesn't care.

"What did you think of the show?"

"I sure wouldn't pay to see it."

"That tank's pretty bleak."

Don's mouth is full, so he nods.

I break off a piece of pizza but don't eat it.

Don swallows. "Look, Lily, I saw what you wanted me to see, and I'm in full agreement. This place exploits dolphins to make money and their living conditions suck. I get it. That still doesn't mean Nori isn't helping Adam, or may, if we keep trying."

"Isn't that exploitation?"

"Yep, but my motivation is my son."

"Do you know how many dolphins have died here?"

"Not a clue."

"Sixty-one. I looked at the Oceanarium's website and came upon an alternate site. It has a list of how many dolphins and seals have died here, including Hugo, their first killer whale, and Carolina Snowball, an albino dolphin. If they kill Nori, what then?"

"I'll feel terrible, but without these people, she would already be dead, and you read that article. If we take her back to the Gulf, she could just as easily die of a lung infection. Here she's got a fighting chance to survive and help your brother at the same time. And while you're feeling bad about these dolphins and that whale, you should remember that they get better health care than most Americans." He squeezes my shoulder, but I shrug his hand off.

"So do inmates in a penitentiary," I mumble.

Don smiles. "You're getting way too emotionally involved with these animals."

I get up. "I'd rather see her die free than live her life in this pit." I've gone a few feet when I realize he dropped the "too emotional" bomb. I turn. "Did you call me too emotional because I'm a girl?"

"I'm sorry, Lily. We'll just have to agree to disagree."

"I'll never agree with you. Every animal in this place—except those pigeons—is at the mercy of people who are only in it for the money."

CHAPTER 34

Later that week, with Adam in school and Don at the hospital, I'm trying to decide whether to mope around the house or call Zoe to see if she wants to do something, when my phone rings. It's Zoe.

"Do you have ESP, too?"

She laughs. "Sometimes. Why?"

"I was just going to call you."

"I don't think it was ESP this time. Mom just suggested this would be a good morning to shop for school clothes. I'm calling to remind you of your promise to go with me so I don't start school dressed like a suffragette."

I laugh. "Let's go to CocoWalk. We could have lunch at Chili's or the Cheesecake Factory, then go to the Gap."

"I've got a better idea. Let's shop first so I don't have to buy a large in everything."

* * * * * *

Zoe looked gorgeous in everything she tried on. By the time we go to lunch with a load of shopping bags, I hate her.

Her new cane is collapsible and is folded next to her plate, so I know that everyone who glances at her when they walk by our table, especially the boys, are looking because she's beautiful, not because she's blind.

"You're quiet," she says.

"I was just wishing you could see how pretty you are."

"I'd rather start with the Grand Canyon or the next full moon."

"I'm shallow, aren't I?"

"No, you're not, and you shouldn't put yourself down. No one is more beautiful than you are."

"I'm not pretty." I tuck the strands of hair that have come loose from my ponytail behind my ear. "My mother was, but I'm not."

"You are to me."

"How? You don't know what I look like."

She smiles. "You're right. I don't have a clue what you look like on the outside. That's how I know you're beautiful, Lily. I can't be misled by appearances."

I swallow the lump in my throat. "Do you want my green peppers?"

"Can't stand them. Will you pick them out of mine, too?"

I laugh, but Zoe's face turns serious.

"Tell me something about your mother," she says. "What was she like?"

A pain spreads through my chest. "She was really nice."

"What's the happiest time you two ever had together?"

"I don't know if I can think of just one." I've picked all the green peppers out of my salad, and start on Zoe's. A woman at the next table glances at me, then away.

"Well?"

"Your salad's safe to eat."

"Thanks."

"I guess it was my tenth birthday. We were down in the Keys at Ocean Reef. You're not going to like this part, but they had two dolphins in a . . . pen. They called it a lagoon, but it wasn't. It was rectangular, the size of an Olympic swimming pool, blasted out of the coral rock. There was a wooden bridge across one end of it, and they kept a little rowboat tied there because people would throw things in with the dolphins and they'd have to row around fishing the stuff out. Mom arranged for the trainer to let me go out in the rowboat. I got to pet the dolphins and give them fish to eat. If I close my eyes, I can still see Momma smiling down at me from the bridge, clapping like mad." I pick at my salad. "Now tell me yours."

"Yours is a nicer story than mine."

"Tell me anyway."

"It was the day they wheeled me into surgery to remove my other eye. Momma was crying her eyes out—" Zoe smiles. "That's a grim expression, isn't it?" She waves her hand like she's shooing a fly. "That's the last time I saw her face, walking beside the gurney, sobbing. Now, even when she's laughing, I have trouble imagining her happy."

"I'm sorry."

"No, don't be. That's not why I'm telling you. My dad understood. He leaned over the gurney and said, 'Look at me, Zoe.' He held my face. 'I love you. Don't forget what love looks like, sweetheart. This is how I will always be looking at you. Remember it.'"

I blot tears with my napkin. "That's the saddest thing I've ever heard."

"Is it? I remember it as a gift. My parents will never grow old in my eyes, and my dad will float there above me, saying I love you for the rest of my life. And you will always remember your mother smiling at you from the bridge."

"I guess I never thought of it like that."

Zoe puts her finger to her lips. "Wait. Listen."

"To what?" I whisper.

Zoe nods her head toward the women sitting at the table next to us.

"Did the kids get to swim with them?" one asks the other.

"No. They were wild dolphins."

"Excuse me," Zoe says without hesitating. "Do you mind? Where were those dolphins?"

"Marco Island. Over by Naples." The woman gives the waiter her credit card.

"Thanks."

The woman nods and smiles, spots Zoe's cane, then looks at me. "It was a tour boat. They took us out and taught my kids to identify dolphins by the cuts and scrapes on their dorsal fins."

"Do you remember the name, by any chance?" I ask.

"I don't. I'm sorry."

After they leave, I say, "We can try to look it up online when we get home."

"What for?"

"I don't know, Zoe. It's got to be more than a coincidence that we overheard her, and that those dolphins aren't anywhere near where the oil spill happened."

"Excuse me." The woman from the other table is back. "I found this in my purse when I was looking for my keys." She hands me a business card. *Dolphin Project, Captain Chris Desmond, Director.*

CHAPTER 35

It's Tuesday. Adam's at school with Suzanne, and Zoe's here. Yesterday, as soon as we got home, we called and left a message for Captain Desmond. Now we're sitting on the steps in the shallow end of the pool, thinking our own thoughts and hoping he'll call back, hoping maybe he can help us find a home for Nori.

A damselfly hitches a ride on a leaf floating in the pool, and I'm watching it. The leaf is near the skimmer and I wonder if the damselfly will lift off before the leaf is sucked into the basket. "You'd better let go."

"What?" Zoe says.

"I'm talking to a damselfly. It's sitting on a leaf that's about to disappear into the skimmer."

"You're not going to let it happen, are you?"

"Of course not." I push off and wade out, expecting the damselfly to go. She doesn't. I catch the stem of the leaf and walk it away from the skimmer. Still she doesn't fly away. "She's letting me take her for a ride," I tell Zoe.

"How do you know it's a girl?"

I laugh. "You're right. It could be a male damselfly." I settle back on the steps with Zoe. "He/she's safe and sound. Wish our other job was that easy."

"Yeah." Zoe shivers. "I'd better get going."

When her mother dropped her off, Zoe told her she'd walk home. Her mother looked at me and shook her head, which sticks me between letting her accomplish the walk on her own, or obeying her mother's wishes. We don't live that far apart, but there's the busy Douglas Road to cross. "I'll walk with you. Want me to?"

"No. It's not like I don't know the way, and I can practice clicking and humming."

"Your mom will be mad if I let you walk home alone. You can still hum and click."

"All right, Mother."

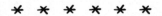

My phone rings when we're a block from Zoe's house. The caller ID reads *Dolphin Project.* "It's him." My heart bounces around in my chest. "Hello?"

"Miss Moran?"

"Yes."

"This is Captain Chris returning your call."

"Yes, sir." I'm completely tongue-tied. Zoe finally elbows me. "Thank you for calling back so quickly."

"You're welcome." There's a long silence. "Did you call to make a reservation?"

"No, sir." I take a deep breath and angle the phone so Zoe can hear, too. "I called because my friend and I are trying to rescue a captive dolphin."

He doesn't laugh. That's a good sign, but he's quiet for so long, I think maybe he hung up. "Captain Chris?"

"Yes, Miss Moran. I'm here. How can I help?"

There's a stop sign on the corner. Some guy blasts his horn at the woman in front of him who has taken a nanosecond too long looking both ways.

"I honestly don't know. We need a place to take her, *if* we can get her released."

"Where was she captured?"

"Panama City."

"That's good. She's a Gulf Coast bottlenose dolphin. They're smaller than the Atlantic bottlenose dolphins. The ones here in Marco are also Gulf Coast dolphins. How old is she?"

"About three, I think."

"And the reason she can't be returned to where she was captured?"

"Her mother died, and they're finding a lot of sick dolphins up there since the oil spill. And she wasn't captured, exactly. She had cancer, but she's cured." I cross my fingers.

"Then I don't see much of a problem," he says.

I find Zoe's hand and squeeze it. Captain Chris is still talking. "Our community of dolphins would readily accept a young dolphin. We're always finding new additions, and we have a lot of moms and calves. She'll fit right in. May I ask who has her and how you think you might get her released?"

"She's at the Bayside Oceanarium—"

"Oh. Well, even so, getting her released shouldn't be too hard. They're not permitted to keep rehabilitated mammals. Once they are cured, they must be returned to the wild."

"Yes, sir. We know. We're working on that."

"You sound kind of young. May I ask?"

I hesitate. He's going to think we're too young to make any difference at all. "I'm twelve."

"Uh-huh."

"Captain Chris, my friend and I can make it happen, if I can convince my dad to help."

"I tell you what. If you succeed, my team will transport her. Just let me know."

"That's wonderful."

"Good luck, young lady."

"Thank you." I hang up, shout, "Yahoo!" and hug Zoe.

CHAPTER 36

Zoe won't let me walk with her any farther than the street in front of her house. She wants to practice her echolocation. I watch her click her way up their gravel driveway and am about to turn for home when I suddenly remember those links she sent me to sites discrediting dolphin-assisted therapy. "Zoe, wait." I run up the driveway and grab her arm. "You called dolphin-assisted therapy a hoax. Remember?"

"Sure. What difference is that going to make?"

"Don's a scientist. What if we show him the proof it doesn't do anything?"

"Oh, my god, Lily. That's it. There was one specifically discrediting the use of DAT to treat autistic kids. I'll send it to you to give to him."

"I've got a better idea. Let's get Sandi Bowman to admit it doesn't help."

"How are you going to do that?"

"I don't know."

"She'll never admit it doesn't work," Zoe says. "She'd be out of a job."

"I know. Wouldn't that be wonderful?"

"How are we even going to get Don and Sandi in the same room?"

"That's the easy part. We make them think the other wants to see them."

Zoe laughs. "I knew you were an evil genius."

✻ ✻ ✻ ✻ ✻ ✻

"Sandi Bowman called." I'm loading dishes into the dishwasher to keep from looking at Don. "She wants to meet with you to discuss Adam's progress."

He's sitting at the kitchen counter, reading the paper. "When?"

"She said whatever's good for you."

"I'd rather do it Saturday, either before or after Adam's session. You can take him to see the stingrays while I talk to her."

I should have known this is when he'd choose. "No."

"No, what?"

"I want to hear what she has to say, too."

"That's fair." He glances at Adam in his play yard with his iPad. "How about Friday? Suzanne can watch Adam. I'll have my office call Sandi and set a time."

We did think of that. When we got to Zoe's, she called Sandi Bowman's office, pretending to be Don's secretary, and told her he wanted a meeting. Sandi will be expecting his call. I just hope she doesn't wonder about a different voice.

I turn to look at him, trying to remember if he's always said Sandi's name in that tone of voice. "You don't have a thing for her, do you?"

He looks startled. "What would make you think that?"

I shrug. "Do you?"

"No. Our lives are complicated enough without—"

Adam starts to babble. We both look at him. I dry my hands and Don folds the newspaper. We're his planets.

CHAPTER 37

The article Zoe sends is from the journal *Autism Research and Treatment*. This article, "Dolphin-Assisted Therapy: Claims versus Evidence," is full of dense scientific language, which I ended up liking even though it took reading it over and over to understand. I tried to imagine my father writing a paper like this, and maybe me, too, one day.

The main points were that, even though DAT has been in use for decades, it's considered an unproven therapy, and its use gets in the way of parents seeking proven treatments. There was a line in the summary that stood out: *It is becoming more evident that reliance on and unrestricted use of unproven therapies for children with autism are hindering the field of autism spectrum disorders treatment and research.*

Zoe and I decide we're not going to practice what I'm going to say to Don and Sandi, or what she's going to say to Don. Neither of us wants to sound stiff and rehearsed. Instead, we are trying not to think about it by racing each other from one end of the pool to the other.

Once she knew where the ladder was, and that the steps in the shallow end are only on one side, she challenged me to a race. She hit the wall pretty hard the first couple of laps, but now she's doing almost perfect flip-turns. I come up laughing and gasping for air after beating her, to find Don standing by the ladder. He watches Zoe make an almost flawless turn and start back the other way.

"How *does* she do that?"

"She's counted how many strokes it takes."

Zoe senses I'm not swimming, upends, and turns around in the water. "Where are you, quitter?"

"Here." I splash her.

She swims to the side of the pool. Her knuckles are scraped up pretty badly.

"Hi, Dr. Moran." She doesn't know where he's standing, just that's he's here.

Don shakes his head. Zoe's a mystery to him. He doesn't get that all her other senses work perfectly well and that water only muffles voices.

"Your knuckles are bleeding," he says. "When you get out, I'll put some Neosporin on them."

"Thanks, they'll be okay. I swam into the wall a couple of times. Hope there are no sharks in here with us."

"Just the one bobbing around with the chlorine tablets in it. You girls have fun." He turns to go back into the house.

"Dr. Moran."

"Yes, Zoe?"

She moves down the side of the pool until she's opposite where she last heard his voice and grips the concrete lip of the deck to the left of where he's standing. *Here we go.* My heart's in my throat.

"Can I tell you something?"

"Sure." He looks at me quizzically, like I know what's coming.

I don't know what she's going to say, only that it will be a pitch to let Nori go.

"I've been blind since I was four—"

"I'm sorry."

"No, sir, that's *not* why I'm telling you." She sighs. "I don't want people treating me differently, or feeling sorry for me. My Braille teacher was right. She told me I'd always be bumping up against other people's low expectations."

"Now I'm sorry for a different reason."

"It's okay. I just wanted to tell you that my parents started out trying to make being blind easier for me by making the world perfectly safe. Lily's been to my house. It's been eight years and all the furniture is still pushed against the walls." She smiles. "Except for one wing-backed chair, my token obstacle."

I explain, "Her mom moves it around so Zoe can practice echolocation."

"How's that going?" Don's not sure of his part in this conversation. He keeps looking at me.

"Fine, thank you. But what I'm trying to say is, if I had let them clear away all the obstacles I've faced since the last surgery, I would never have learned to overcome any of them."

I'm glad Zoe can't see Don's amused little smile. "It's only because they love you."

"Love can cripple, you know."

His smile disappears. "I do know that."

"I came home from the hospital after losing my other eye, determined to be the greatest blind kid ever, only to find my parents had cleared the dinette set out of the kitchen and set up a fenced-in area for me, full of soft, safe toys."

"Are you trying to compare that with Adam's play yard?"

She'd forgotten about the pen in our living room, and it throws her off balance.

"No. I—I . . ."

I'm sitting waist deep on the second step in the shallow end of the pool. I swim over to join Zoe. "I think she wants to tell you that too much love—"

"No, that's not it." She flaps her hand at me. "There can't be too much love, but it has to be the letting-go kind."

"Zoe, you were a blind four-year-old. What did you expect your parents to do?"

"Help me find my way. Instead they put me in a cage where I would be safe. It was terrifying. To navigate, I have to rely on the pictures that form in my head, and on my memory. In that pen, I couldn't explore or create anything new."

"I'm not doing that to Adam."

"Dr. Moran, I'm not talking about Adam. I'm talking about Nori."

"Sorry." Don holds his hands up. "I've already told Lily I would think about it. That has to satisfy you two for right now."

"We found a place for her," I blurt out. "Over at Marco Island."

Zoe doesn't give him time to do anything but blink. "Please listen, Dr. Moran. I've thought a lot about this.

Just like Adam, I have to live with what I can and cannot do. I still want to be the greatest blind kid, maybe change the way people see the blind and change their expectations about what we can accomplish. And I admit I have an advantage over Adam. I can tell you how I feel. If he could do that, he'd tell you that he loves Nori—loves her enough not to want her penned up for his sake. My blindness could have been a prison for my parents if I let them pad the world for me. You don't want that for someone you love. Do you understand?"

"It's not the same, Zoe."

"Yes, sir, it is." Her voice is shrill. "We don't want to steal the lives of those we love."

I put my hand on her arm.

Don looks at me. The skin on his face is slack like a sail with no wind, and there's something about the way he's standing with his arms at his sides that feels familiar, and not in a good way. Then I remember.

✳ ✳ ✳ ✳ ✳ ✳

July 29, two years ago, Adam and I were in the pool. I was clinging to the end of an inflatable raft, scissor-kicking to propel Adam through the water. His little feet were on my shoulders. A nanny, whose name I can't remember, sat in the shade reading *People* magazine. When I turned, Don was standing near the deep end, arms loose at his sides, head down. I remember the sound my kicks made as the water lapped against the tile. There was a strange car in the driveway.

"Whose car is that?"

His head came up, and he looked over his shoulder. "It's a rental."

"Where's Mom?"

His face went from no expression to a look like he'd been stabbed. "Get out of the pool, Lily."

There's no way I could have imagined what he was going to say, but the change in his face caused my heart to thunder and the water to feel like ice. "Where's Momma?" I screamed.

* * * * * *

That same old sun-bleached raft was blowing around the pool when Zoe and I first got in. I pulled it out before we started racing. It's lying on the grass. It never would have occurred to me that Don might also recognize the sameness of this moment, not until I see him look at it, then up at the blue, blue sky.

CHAPTER 38

Sandi Bowman comes around her desk and extends her hand. Don takes it. "Libby." She nods at me.

I don't bother to correct her, but Don says, "My daughter's *name* is Lily."

"Sorry." Sandi closes her eyes and thumps her forehead with the side of her fist, then gives me an apologetic, horse-toothed smile. "I'm horrible with names."

I smile at her. I can be insincere, too.

"Sit you two, sit. What can I do for you, Don?"

Don's confused. "I thought you wanted to talk to me."

"I'm always happy—" Sandi blinks. "It was your secretary who called me."

"That's funny. Lily said—"

My heart's flip-flopping around in my chest like a fish out of water, and my hands start to shake. I jam them between my thighs and the seat. "I called Sandi," I say to Don, keeping Zoe out of it, and say to Sandi, "And I told Don that you had called."

Don pushes his chair back and stands. "I'm sorry about this," he says. "Let's go." He heads for the door.

"Not until I finish." My voice quivers. I sit up straight and take a deep breath. "You owe it to me to listen."

"Oh, Don, let her talk." Sandi gives me a patronizing smile. "I'm sure, as Adam's sister, she has legitimate concerns about his progress."

"My *concern* is for Nori. I'd like you to show my step . . . my dad and me some statistics on how beneficial dolphin-assisted therapy is." This is when it occurs to me she might have some. I didn't look at the date on that journal article.

"What kind of statistical information?" She retreats behind her desk, leans, and straightens her nameplate before sitting down. She's dotted the *i* in her name with a tiny red sticker-heart.

"What do you have?"

Sandi leans back and forms a church steeple with the tips of her fingers. "Well, sweetie, let's see. The first pilot studies of dolphin-assisted therapy took place at Ocean World in Fort Lauderdale in 1978 and 1979. Since then, research has shown that two weeks of DAT is just as good if not better than other traditional treatments. Reports indicate that a two-week program significantly increases language, speech, and motor skills among children with various disabilities when compared to the more conventional speech or physical therapy programs that can last six months or more."

"I'd like to see that." I turn to Don. "Wouldn't you?"

Don stands with his back to the door. He doesn't move or answer.

I wish Zoe was here. I'd be braver. Instead, I close my eyes for a second and see Momma on the bridge at Ocean Reef, then I turn to Don. "Wouldn't you like to know that there's proof this will help Adam? Some evidence? Anything at all?"

He walks over and sits down.

I turn back to Sandi, whose smirky condescending little smile is gone.

This is it. I win or lose depending on what I say next. "I don't think this is doing anything more for Adam than swimming with any dolphin would do—" I look at Don. "Or playing with the stingrays, or buying him a puppy. It's fun and it makes him happy."

"Don't you think that's important?" Sandi says.

"I love seeing my brother happy, but not at the price of Nori's freedom."

"Look," she says to Don, "I've had years of experience working with dolphins and disabled children. I know it helps. EEGs of brain activity confirm that dolphins have a relaxing influence on people, and that lends itself to significant progress for children with disabilities."

Don's coming back to her desk and sitting down has made her nervous. Now she thinks she's got to argue her case for his benefit instead of mine. I wish I was as sure. If she starts with medical jargon and acronyms, I won't know what she's saying. I bet she's counting on that. I already don't know what to say next, and out of the corner of my eye I can see Don watching me. Sink or swim. "How does being relaxed help an autistic kid?" *Lame. Lame.*

Don smiles ever so slightly, and Sandi takes it to mean she hasn't lost him. "The theory is that it will result in an increase in their attention to stimuli in the environment and lead to enhanced learning, motor skills, language, and memory."

I glom on to one word. "It's a theory?"

"Well . . . the sample size is rather small and it's a bit hard to find concrete data due to the absence of a control group, but personally I feel strongly that DAT is superior to traditional methods of intervention."

My insides light up. She just put down schools like Cutler Academy, the accepted best option for autistic kids.

Don clears his throat. I hold my breath. "You do know that without a control group, it's impossible to rule out the placebo effect, and therefore there is no proof it does anything."

Sandi stiffens. "Admittedly, there's still a lot of work to be done."

"How much are you planning to charge other families for this program?"

If I were her, I'd have been suspicious of that question, but she thinks Don wants to know what a great deal he's getting. Her smile suggests he's going to be pleased with the answer.

"Once Nori's training is complete, we'll provide five forty-minute sessions for twenty-six hundred dollars. That's average for this kind of treatment."

Don smiles at her. "And what does that include?"

"Exactly what we've been doing with your son. An orientation session to make sure the child is comfortable with dolphins. Then he or she starts the series of therapeutic sessions where the child is allowed to play with the dolphins for a short time either from the dock or by going in the water with them. During that play time the children can touch or kiss the dolphin, dance in a circle with the dolphin, or ride on the dolphin by holding on to the dorsal fin."

Sandi stops to take a breath. Don doesn't say anything, so she plows on.

"It's been suggested that ultrasound emitted by dolphins through echolocation clicks has a healing effect on the human body. This is one of the most popular theories behind DAT."

"What evidence is there to support this theory?" Don asks.

He's with me now, I can tell. I don't move, or breathe.

"Well, admittedly it's mostly anecdotal."

"So you do know," Don says, "that a human interacting with a dolphin differs from medical use of therapeutic ultrasound, which calls for repeated application at a specific intensity and duration?"

"Yes. Yes. I know that." Her tone is wary.

He nods. "So, really, there's no proof at all that dolphin-assisted therapy is anything more than a swim-with-dolphin program and lucrative employment for a therapist."

Don sighs, a letting-go kind of sigh, then stands and puts his hand on my shoulder. When I turn and look up at him, he kisses my forehead.

"Dr. Moran, I hope you'll continue to give this therapy the chance it deserves."

"Get your vet on the phone."

"May I ask why?

"I'm rescinding my authorization to keep Nori."

The color drains from her face. "Are you sure?"

"Quite."

"But why? I thought your son—" She has to search her mind for Adam's name. "I thought Adam was doing so well."

"He is doing as well as can be expected for a kid with severe autism, but my daughter"—he takes my hand—"has shown me the error in my thinking. This is not a suitable place for any dolphin to live, and I'm not going to let you keep Nori."

CHAPTER 39

Don and Suzanne are in the front of the car; Zoe and I are in the back with Adam between us. We're following the truck carrying Nori across the Tamiami Trail. Three employees of the Dolphin Project—Kent, James, and Kristen—came over from Marco Island to pick her up. Kent is driving, and James and Kristen are in the back with Nori, who's in a foam-padded crate. Kristen's keeping Nori's skin wet with a sponge, and calming her.

We're about two hours into the pretty quiet drive—except for Adam's whining, and turning every once in a while to slap my shoulder with both hands like I'm a drum. We all jump when we hear Kent's voice crackle over the walkie-talkie he gave us. "We've heard from Chris. The *Dolphin Explorer* is in the water and following a subadult group not far from the Jolley Bridge. Over."

"What does 'subadult' mean?" Don radios back, then adds, "Over."

"Nori's age group. Between four and eight."

Adam doesn't know Nori's in the truck, and has been babbling and slapping me, his knees, or Zoe's since we left home. Nothing I try—including pointing out alligators in the canal—has kept him quiet. It's making for a very long drive. When he hears Nori's name, he stops yammering and listens.

"Thanks," Don says, and glances in the rearview mirror.

"Roger that. We'll be turning toward Marco in another few miles."

A few minutes later, we see their truck turn left and the walkie-talkie crackles. "There's a boat waiting for us at the base of Jolley Bridge. Just follow us. Over."

"Roger," Don says.

I duck my head so Don doesn't see me grin at his growing comfort with the walkie-talkie language.

The Jolley Bridge is high. Adam leans down, sees it, and begins to make sounds like a puppy crying, a prelude to screaming his head off. But Kent's right turn signal flashes and he turns off the highway at the base of the bridge and drives to the end of a gravel parking lot. He pulls up next to a path to the water's edge and cuts the engine. We pull in beside him and get out of the car.

Kent comes over. "The boat to take us to meet Chris is on the beach at the end of this trail. Chris just radioed. The dolphin group he's following is in the Marco River about two miles from here."

James and Kristen wait for Kent to lower the tailgate before jumping down. "We're going to need a hand." Kent signals Don.

Don takes up one side of the sling Nori is in, then the four of them lift her up and out of the truck.

They carry Nori to the guardrail, lift her over, and carry her down the path. Suzanne follows with Adam, who sees Nori for the first time and stares like he can't believe his eyes.

There is a gap in the guardrail, but if we cross there to reach the path through the sea grapes, I'll have to lead Zoe across blocks of limestone that form a breakwater. The boulders are different sizes, heights, and spacing. I can't imagine Zoe crossing them without breaking an ankle.

Kent appears. "Need some help?"

I say, "Yes," and Zoe says, "We do not."

He smiles. "Go back down the road twenty yards. There's beach access and you can walk back up to the boat."

There are branches to duck on the trail along the beach, so Zoe walks with her hand on my shoulder. By the time we reach the boat, they have Nori lying on the deck on top of what looks like an inflated blue mattress. The sling has been pulled from beneath her and rolled up. Kristen fills a bucket with water and Don helps her lift it into the boat. She ladles a full 7-Eleven Slurpee cup over Nori, careful to miss her blowhole.

Adam is squirming to get out of the grip Suzanne has on him. "Who's that?" She turns so Adam can see over her shoulder. He squeaks, starts to giggle, and holds his arms out to get close to Nori.

Don helps Zoe board the boat and takes Adam from Suzanne.

I climb onboard.

Don asks Kent if Adam can sit with Nori.

"First, let James get a few pictures of that nick in the top of her dorsal fin and that scar on her beak. That will help identify her in the future."

James circles Nori, snapping pictures, reviews them, then nods. "These will do."

The moment his feet touch the deck, Adam falls to his knees, crawls over, and stretches out beside Nori on the mattress, his face an inch from her eye. He murmurs to her and strokes her head.

Kent starts the engine; Kristen pushes us off and hops aboard. The engine is loud in a way that would normally have Adam shrieking, but he doesn't notice.

Don's watching Adam. I know he's not convinced that releasing Nori is the right thing to do as far as his son is concerned, but it's too late to turn back now. He senses me watching him and looks up. I expect he's pretty mad at me and Zoe right now, but I can't tell from his expression, which is flat and unemotional. He looks again at Adam, then turns his back to watch the water.

I can still see the bridge when Kent slows the engine, picks up a pair of binoculars, and focuses on a flock of gulls above a group of dolphins feeding at the surface. A catamaran is following them. We motor slowly toward them until we're alongside the cat.

A man I assume is Captain Chris cuts the boat's engine. The only sound is the slap of waves against the hull of the boat, the blows of the feeding dolphins, and the cries of the gulls.

There are introductions all around. He takes my hand and pats it. "Congratulations, young lady." He smiles and turns to Don. "The dolphins in this group are moms with their calves—a good group for Nori to first be exposed to. I don't think we'll do better." He looks at Adam lying beside Nori, whispering nonsense words. His lips compress, then he says, "It's time, if you're ready."

Don lifts Adam, wrapping one arm around his waist and the other pinning his legs.

Adam squirms, tries to kick, and begins to cry.

"Adam." I step in front of Don, put my hands on either side of Adam's face, and make him look at me. "It's Nori's turn."

This stumps him, and he quiets.

"Nori is going over to play with those dolphins. See them?" I point. "You have to let these people put her in the water." I hold my arms out and Don hands Adam to me. "Dad's going to help lift her over the side."

James sits on the gunnel, swings his legs around, and drops into the water. Don, Kent, Chris, and Kristen lift Nori over the gunnel and put the mattress in the water. It floats on the surface with Nori in the center. James holds it steady until Kristen slides into the water. They move to the front, one on either side. Kristen looks up at us. "Ready?"

The five dolphins are about twenty yards away and completely ignoring us.

"Give me a second," I say. I've got Adam by the straps of his overalls, which is all that's keeping him from climbing over the side. "No, honey." My voice cracks with emotion. "It's Nori's turn."

Adam looks at me. There's the pain and confusion.

" 'Little Dolphin wants to play,' " I say—a quote from his *Little Dolphin* puppet book.

At the same time, three of the five dolphins surface and blow. Adam watches them, then looks at Nori.

"Are you ready, Adam?" I hold up four fingers, then fold them one at a time. "Four, three, two, one."

Kristen and James push down on the front of the mattress and Nori floats off.

She lies in the water for a moment, then turns toward the boat and rolls on her side.

"You know how it's done. Tell her to go play with her friends."

Adam's little brow creases.

"Go on. Send her to play with those dolphins."

Adam lifts his arm, bends it at the elbow, then straightens it out, finger pointing.

Nori flops sideways, gives a pump of her tail, and zips off to joins the other dolphins.

EPILOGUE

For whatever reason, Adam has never said Nori's name, or shown in any way that he misses her. It's as though time and distance, for the bond they share, are meaningless. Don doesn't think Adam has the emotional ability to miss her. I try to think that's autism's gift—not to miss a person or a thing so much your heart breaks.

When the accident that killed my mother first happened, she died a hundred times a day, and I blamed myself. She was on her way home from taking her best friend, Judy, to the airport. She'd asked me to come along, but I wanted to stay home and play in the pool. I kept thinking that if I'd gone with her, we would have stopped for ice cream and she would have come to that intersection *after* that drunk driver ran the stop sign. Or I would have gotten out to hug Judy good-bye and that few seconds would have made the difference.

I don't blame myself anymore. It's just what happened, and I'm finally able to think of her and not have that ache spread through me. I think she's at ease now, too, knowing I'm the person she would have wanted me to be and that Adam and Don and I are a family.

Adam will turn five on January 20, but since he doesn't know one day from the next, we are celebrating this Saturday. Don is taking us to Marco Island to find Nori. At least, we hope to see her. Captain Chris told Don he's seen her lots of times in the last five months, but no guarantees. Either way, there will be lots of dolphins for Adam to squeak at.

Suzanne, her son, daughter-in-law, and new grandbaby—a little girl they named Suzanne and call Baby Suz—are going on the boat with us. And Zoe, of course. If it hadn't been for Zoe, we might never have convinced Don to set Nori free.

Suzanne lives with us now. Don added a "granny unit" over by the hedge between our house and Mrs. Walden's. Suzanne moved in a month ago.

The drive to Marco Island is two and a half hours. Suzanne suggested getting earphones for Adam's iPad. He watches one of his dolphin movies on the drive over.

At the Marco Island Marina, we find the *Dolphin Explorer* booth and are directed to the dock, where we spot Captain Chris waving to us from one of the slips. With him is a large dog who bounds off the catamaran to greet us.

"That's Riley," Chris says. "He's an Australian Labradoodle, and he loves dolphins."

Under Don's watchful eye, Riley sniffs Adam and licks his face, which makes Adam giggle.

The *Dolphin Explorer* is a thirty-six-foot-long catamaran with room for twenty-eight passengers at fifty-eight dollars a person, but Don chartered it, so for this trip, it's the eight of us. Kent, the guy who drove the truck the day we released Nori, gives safety instructions, points out where the life jackets are located, and reminds us we are to stay seated when the boat's running. "We use the clock to share the location of the dolphins," he says, "so if you spot one, refer to its location as if the bow is twelve o'clock."

As we push off from the dock, Captain Chris looks at Don and says, "There will be no getting in the water with the dolphins. Is that clear?"

We nod—except for Adam. He hears "dolphin," squeezes out a raspberry, and flaps his hand. Captain

Chris kneels in front of him. "I need a lookout to help me find the dolphins. Will you do that for me?"

Adam doesn't answer or look at Captain Chris, but he marches to the port-side railing and waves his palm in front of his own face at the receding dock.

Chris watches him with sad eyes and says to me, "That makes perfect sense, doesn't it? He *is* the one leaving."

I nod and want to hug him.

We're only ten minutes out when Zoe hears a blow and calls, "Dolphins at five o'clock." In the same instant, Riley barks and scrambles from the bow to the stern, where Don is helping Adam climb onto the back bench to watch them. Riley jumps up to stand beside Adam.

Suzanne sits on the other rear bench, holding Baby Suz, who is startled by Riley and starts to cry. Don reaches and takes her from Suzanne. He jiggles her and points out the two dolphins that broke off from the group. I don't think Don has held a baby since Adam was born. Suzanne and I look at each other and smile.

One of the dolphins races along in our stern wake, but the other, with Riley barking his approval, leaps into the air and spins before crashing back into the water. It does this four or five times. Adam squeals and giggles. When they break off and disappear, he strokes Riley's head.

A few minutes later, another group of dolphins approaches from under the Jolley Bridge.

"Are those the same dolphins?" I ask.

Captain Chris shakes his head. "Different." He has to shout over the roar of the two huge outboard engines.

I was sure I'd recognize Nori when I saw her, but if she's among these, I can't tell. I glance at Captain Chris and see him smile.

"Here come more." Don picks Adam up, but this time when Adam sees them, he doesn't laugh or giggle. He stares, and holds his arms out. When he can't get away from Don, he starts to buck until he kicks him hard just below his kneecap. Don grunts and puts him down, but keeps a vicelike grip on his Kid Keeper leash.

The dolphins, six of them this time, surf our wake, porpoising in and out of the wave. My heart pounds. I want Nori to be with them, and Adam thinks she is, but I don't believe for a minute that, if she is, she'll recognize us. It's been five months.

When the dolphins tire of chasing through the water after us, five zip away, but one stays, swimming alongside. Now there's no doubt. It's Nori. Kent flips through the notebook full of pictures until he comes to the pictures James took the day we set her free. The nick in her dorsal fin and the scar on her beak are the same.

Captain Chris pulls the power and puts the engine in neutral.

Adam has his fingers through the metal grillwork that caps the sides of the catamaran. He rocks back and forth, mumbling something.

Zoe touches my arm. "Lily, do you hear what Adam is saying?"

"I can't tell."

"The words aren't clear, but from the rhythm, the cadence, I think it's his *Little Dolphin* story."

"His book?"

Zoe leans near Adam and says, " 'Someone must have heard his call!' "

" 'Here comes a friend,' " Adam says, clear as a bell.

" 'They'll have a ball,' " Zoe and I answer.

Nori upends on the port side of the boat and lets out a high-pitched whistle.

"That's one excited dolphin," Chris says.

Nori dives. The water isn't as clear as the tank in Miami, but it's clear enough to see the bubble ring she's blown and is pushing toward us. I pick Adam up and stand him on the railing.

"Is that Nori?" I ask him.

Zoe claps her hands. "Is it?"

"Yes, and she's bringing Adam a bubble ring."

Adam jumps, folding his legs up, only to dangle mid-air with my arms around him. He's heavy. If Don hadn't reached out and grabbed him, he would have been in the water.

Captain Chris opens the gate to the bow. "Go on. Let him pet his dolphin."

Don puts Adam down. I hold on to him and the two of us lie on the decking and hang over the water between the two hulls. Adam clicks and squeaks and shrieks with laughter when Nori pops up in front of him. She presses her beak to his cheek, then whistles and makes popping sounds through her blowhole before opening her mouth to let Adam tickle her tongue.

We hang out over the water until Nori leaves to join a group of dolphins swimming by. Adam watches her go, and lets me pick him up and carry him back through the gate. Captain Chris starts the motor and steers us toward Keewaydin Island, where we'll go ashore to look for shells, walk the beach, and let Adam burn off extra energy before we head home.

On the way, Adam stands on the bench at the stern and watches our wake. Riley joins him there—two dolphin lovers side by side.

＊　＊　＊　＊　＊　＊

On the island, Zoe sits waist deep in the water. She's looking for shells, too. She digs them out of the sand, rinses what she finds, and inspects each one, inside and out, with her fingers.

I stand nearby with my toes digging in the warm sand, listening to the waves make little hissing sounds as they roll in, and watch Adam and Riley run up the beach and down the beach. Flocks of small shore birds feed at the water's edge, following each receding wave to probe the sand quickly for what the wash has turned up, before dashing ashore ahead of the next little wave.

Suzanne and her family are down the beach and letting the baby splash in a puddle of warm water left by the outgoing tide.

Riley sees Nori first and barks. Adam turns, sees her, and dashes into the surf. Don and Kent run in after him to keep him from swimming out to meet her.

"That's quite a bond those two have." Captain Chris pushes his cap back on his head. "I suppose if your brother sat in the water, I couldn't stop the dolphin from coming to him."

"How can she? It's so shallow."

"She'll manage. I've seen dolphins chase fish onto a beach, swim in, and pluck them off the sand."

"Thank you." I run to the water's edge and wade out to where Don and Adam stand. I sit in the water and put Adam in my lap. Nori propels herself in beside us, and Adam puts his cheek against Nori's forehead. I glance up at Don and smile, then splash water on Nori to keep her back wet.

We're only there a few minutes before Captain Chris calls, "We got to get going, folks. Tide's going out."

"Adam, it's time for Nori to join her new family."

Adam studies my face, looks at Nori, and back at me. I'm not sure what to expect. Tears at least, or confusion, but he doesn't react at all.

"Can you send her away?"

He turns, swings his arm like a dolphin trainer, and points to open water.

Nori arches her back and works her way into deeper water.

Adam waves his backward bye-bye.

Nori rolls on her side, waves a pectoral fin, and disappears. Adam and I wade ashore. We pick our way across the shells that line the water's edge, join Don, and turn for a last look at Nori. Her head is out of the water. She bobs it, then dives. A moment later she sails out of the water. Adam laughs, grabs my hand and Don's, then bends his knees and leaps into the air. Don and I together hold him aloft.

Acknowledgments

With gratitude to the teachers and therapists at the Redwood School: Jeannie Stickel, Amy Stephens, Melody Ulrich, Shea Elledge, and Lisa Comarsh; Texas A&M faculty: Josue Delgado and Dr. Joanne Mansell. Thanks to Mark Palmer at Dolphin Project / Earth Island Institute in Berkeley for taking my many calls. Thank you to Anne Eaton Kemp and Pat Dunbar for their keen-eyed reading. A special thanks to Christina Zecca, who generously shared her autistic son's struggles. Peeing in a tuna can would never have occurred to me; thank you, Steve Sapontzis, who introduced me to JAWS and other aspects of his sightless world. Thanks to Spencer Williams, Jane Phinney, and Randy and Carolina Phinney for their guidance and hospitality on my research trips to Florida; as always, my writing group, the Mixed Pickles: Norma Watkins, Katherine Brown, Jill Myers, Patty Joslyn, and Kate Erickson. I'm grateful to Suzanne's daughter, Elisa Hartman, who permitted me to share my grief over the loss of her mother while coping with her own. Thanks to Laurie Arnez for putting me in touch with Captain Chris Desmond, and his crew, Kent Morse, James, and Kristen. Thank you to Ellen Duda and Starr Baer at Scholastic. This book wouldn't exist on any level if not for Emily Seife's dream, her perseverance, and her editing skills.

Note from the Author

While the story here is invented, I did a lot of research to create Adam's character and to inform Nori's situation.

This is a partial list of the readings I did as I prepared to write this book:

"Dolphin-Assisted Therapy: Claims versus Evidence"
Britta L. Fiksdal, Daniel Houlihan, and
Aaron C. Barnes
www.hindawi.com/journals/aurt/2012/839792/
A thorough study of the evidence behind dolphin-assisted therapy.

"Like a Bat, Blind Man Uses Sound to 'See'"
Katie Moisse
abcnews.go.com/Health/MindMoodNews/blind
-man-echolocation/story?id=13684073
The story of a man who uses echolocation.

"Dolphins Suffering from Lung Disease Due to BP Gulf Oil Spill"
ecowatch.com/2013/12/18/dolphins-suffering
-from-disease-bp-gulf-oil-spill/
A look at the effects of the oil spill on Gulf dolphins.

"Reaching My Autistic Son through Disney"
Ron Suskind
www.nytimes.com/2014/03/09/magazine/reaching
-my-autistic-son-through-disney.html?_r=0
An article adapted from Ron Suskind's *Life, Animated*,
about how he and his wife reached their autistic son
through his fascination with Disney movies.

Save Lolita
www.savelolita.com
A website protesting the captivity of a killer whale.

—Ginny Rorby